The Collar
and the
Bracelet

The Collar
and the
Bracelet

Yahya Taher Abdullah

Translated by Samah Selim

The American University in Cairo Press
Cairo   New York

First published in 2008 by
The American University in Cairo Press
113 Sharia Kasr el Aini, Cairo, Egypt
420 Fifth Avenue, New York, NY 10018
www.aucpress.com

The Collar and the Bracelet was first published in Arabic as *al-Tawq wa-l-iswira* in 1975. "From the Dark Blue, A Story," "The Story of Abd al-Halim Effendi and What the Silly Woman Did to Him," "The Story of the Village Maiden," "An Embroidered Tale," and "A Melodramatic Story" were first published in Arabic in *Hikayat li-l-amir hatta yanam* in 1978. "The Song of Elia the Lover," "Mr. Sayyid Ahmad Sayyid," "The Ghoul," "Tears," "Fear," "Death," "Be a Good Egyptian: Be the Master," and "The Messenger" were first published in Arabic in *al-Raqsa al-mubaha* in 1983.

Dar el Kutub No. 20186/07
ISBN 978 977 416 145 2

Dar el Kutub Cataloging-in-Publication Data

Abdullah, Yahya Taher
     The Collar and the Bracelet: and other stories / Yahya Taher
     Abdullah; translated by Samah Selim. — Cairo: The American
     University in Cairo Press, 2008
     p.   cm.
     ISBN 977 416 145 9
     1. Arabic fiction   I. Title   II. Selim, Samah (trans.)
     813

1 2 3 4 5 6   12 11 10 09 08

Designed by Fatiha Bouzidi/AUC Press Design Center
Printed in Egypt

Contents

The Collar and
the Bracelet

Chapter One

The Absent One

With the men, Mustafa departed for the Sudan while still a boy. A year passed, and the twelfth month of the second year came to its end without news of the absent beloved.

Hazina's Thoughts, a Mother's Heart

Hazina's thoughts are with her son, there, in faraway lands. Her right ear—the one that hears—is here with the cooing doves that cry, He is the Lord of Creation! The light deserted her right eye two years ago. Her left eye watches: Bikhit al-Bishari stretched out on the stone bench that circles the trunk of the doum tree. (At the end of those long years that had passed like a boat lifted from a spot of sun and deposited in a spot of shade, he took to gazing at the sun as it raced through the sky and shouting at times, "I want the sun!" and at others, "I want the shade!" Thus, all day long. Thus, the day passes. Thus, the days that make up a life pass. She and her daughter carry the boat from the sun to the shade and from the shade to the sun. He is her legally wedded husband and the father of Mustafa and Fahima.)

Her two hands stroke—here, the spindle which never ceases turning and gathering up the thread. Her thoughts are there, with the absent one in faraway foreign lands.

Bikhit al-Bishari in a Waking Monologue

The lamp oil burns low and the long, dark night approaches. Oh, these aches and pains of old age! Sleep eludes me and I can't control my bladder anymore. Feeble-minded Hazina sees evil omens in an overturned shoe, in the breeze that carries off a garlic husk, in the foot that carelessly steps on a discarded crust of bread. It's not her fault. She is a woman after all, and the men of the house are resigned to affliction. Her thoughts are with the boy and the boy is in distant Sudan. The boy's heart is made of stone and I'm the invalid of the house. I want to sleep—I crave sleep. If I sleep a long, deep sleep without dreams or nightmares I'll go straight up to the merciful God—I, the Muslim—and I'll be rid of these aches and of this hateful life. I'll go to heaven.

If I had some tobacco, I'd smoke to pass this leaden time that I can no longer bear.

Of the Wisdom of Night, Master of Villages

I

A shooting star fell through the lofty blue sky and flared out before reaching earth. If it were to touch man or beast or field or even jinn, they would be instantly transformed into cinder.

II

Mustafa is the younger by two and a half years but he is Fahima's master: he beats her and she loves him. The mother does not object and the father does not object. Mustafa protects Fahima and instills the fear of disgrace in her. Mustafa is a man and Fahima is a girl. A girl is a long-trained white dress.

She must gather up the hem of her dress and pick her way carefully along the muddy, refuse-strewn road.

The Girl is Anxious and Night is
the Friend of Reverie

She is the daughter of the mother and the father, and he is her brother. She loves him and he certainly returns that love. At first, she used to cry. As time passed, she began to provoke him into beating her. Then she would only pretend to cry, and she would hurl insults at him. And so the fire within him would spark and flare and his blows grow violent. His man-face would redden with warm pulsing blood and the veins of his neck dilate till they seemed on the point of exploding.

O Lord, protect us from his anger, he who used to climb Grabana the Christian's date palm at night right under the nose of the sleeping watchman! Mustafa stole the dates and sold them to buy tobacco. Fahima never told Hazina, her mother, nor Bikhit, her father, that Mustafa smoked. And even now, they don't know it. Mustafa is afraid of his mother and of his ailing father.

He used to swim in the irrigation canal with the other boys behind his parents' back. They forbade him to swim in the canal. They feared that he would drown, or that a lovely sprite would steal his heart and lead him down into the blue deep.

He stripped and stood naked as on the day he was born. Fahima followed him secretly, without a word to her parents. Could she have spoken even if she so desired? And even now, neither he nor they know. He went outside, relieved himself, and came back into the house. Fahima crept along under veil of night. The mixture of urine and earth gave off the smell of rotted green sycamore fruit. Fahima would secretly sniff the odor of Mustafa's sweat—the odor of the dirty clothes that had gathered up his body—before washing them.

And here is the girl, gazing up at her shooting star with trembling heart: how far away it is, that deep blue sky. And how terrifying you are in spite of the distance that separates us, my dear, absent brother.

The Sixth Month of the Third Year

The gypsy muttered something that set the rings in her nose and ears dancing, and she drew a cloth purse from her basket. She untied the purse, revealing a pile of sand and stones. Hazina offered her two eggs. "Three," the gypsy said and grinned at Hazina. Her silver tooth shone. "The girl is comely . . . like the full moon," she mumbled slyly. Hazina stared at the dancing rings, and she thought, "I won't let her steal my daughter away, this woman with no hearth of her own, child- and chicken-thief, mistress of trickery. I won't let her steal my daughter. But she knows how to speak with the stones." "Three eggs it is," she replied. "Hmph!"

What the Stones Said
and What the Gypsy Said

I see him. There he is. Come closer Mother, and look.

A train of black iron, throwing up smoke and dust and fields and houses and families.

And a ship rocked by water and sped by wind. The hills are black and the sand on either side is yellow. Kings walk the country. Sun passes through sky and water. In the water is a moon and in the sky is a moon: it's the days and months, Auntie.

Rejoice, Mother! On the day of the eighth sun your boy-child set safe foot on land.

News

From the river Fahima returned. She struck the wooden door of the house with her foot and cried, "Mother, Mother!" Anger gripped Hazina. She heard the wooden door bang against the mud wall. She heard Fahima's shouts and the clatter of the clay jar as it fell from Fahima's head and shattered into pieces. "The idiot," Hazina muttered. Al-Bishari kicked the covers off his face. "Does the girl think she's at market, howling over rotten produce?" he shouted. "What's going on? Has the Day of Judgment come upon us?"

"A letter has arrived from Abd al-Hakam to his family," Fahima yelled.

"The girl still thinks she's at the market! Who's this Abd al-Hakam, and what's he got to do with us?"

"Abd al-Hakam is the son of Tafida, daughter of Ali, Mustafa's companion in his exile," Hazina said.

"You mean Abd al-Hakam Taha? Taha al-Hajjaj Muhammad's son? Abd al-Hakam, son of Taha Muhammad?" And then he asked, "And Mustafa? What news of Mustafa?"

Hazina looked at the broken jar and a shadow passed over her heart. This is the harbinger. She paused while putting on her outdoor cloak. "I'll go. I'll find out from them."

Happy Tidings

In Abd al-Hakam's letter to his family, there are greetings from Mustafa to his family. Now Hazina's mind is at rest. She settled down with the women and with Tafida, daughter of Ali, mother of Abd al-Hakam. She ate dried dates, drank tea, and listened to five tons of talk about the men, about the letter, and about money (such daydreams!) and she repeated it all, parrot-like, to al-Bishari and Fahima.

"They sleep in rows upon rows of tents. The good earth needs water. They dig canals and lay railroad tracks. Black soldiers who jabber in the tongue of the red Englishmen share their tents and their work. The men hear the distant howls of wild animals at night. The snakes are enormous, winged, their necks ringed with black collars, and scorpions also abound. Sudan is the land of saints and of the virtuous. Sudan is the land of magic and amulets and of the long-awaited Savior. Some of its people prefer human flesh, but they inhabit the forests far from the men."

Praise and Thanks Be to God

At Mansur al-Sadiq's shop, Hazina bartered six eggs for a large packet of sweet tobacco emblazoned with a star. She took the packet and gave it to Yusuf Salim, Shaykh Musa's collector of offerings. Hazina asked Yusuf Salim to give the packet of tobacco to the blessed shaykh and to ask him to pray for Mustafa's safety in faraway foreign lands.

A Discussion

Bikhit al-Bishari said to Hazina, "Yusuf Salim will keep the tobacco for himself," and he thought, "A large packet of tobacco emblazoned with a star."

"Bikhit al-Bishari wanted me to give him the tobacco," Hazina thought, "so that he could order me to light the firewood and the girl to fill the pipe with water, so that he could set his pipe singing and blow smoke out of his mouth and nostrils like a real king. Yusuf Salim is a good man."

"Yusuf Salim is a good man," she said to Bikhit. "The shaykh chose him from amongst the whole village to be his deputy. He didn't choose you, did he?"

Bikhit al-Bishari contemplated Hazina. He knew her inside and out from long intimacy. "Hazina is a troublemaker. Now she's after my bones. She wants to dig her claws into my flesh. I'm the man of the house. When I was young and strong I knew how to shut her up. When night falls, I'll weep under my covers. If Hazina or Fahima wake up from the noise, I'll scream at them, 'Leave me alone! I'm mourning my affliction. Let me be!'"

"Shaykh Musa is a blessed man," Fahima said in order to break the silence between the mother and the father. She thought to herself, "When he was the same age as me he threw his cloak onto the water and it floated. He sat on it and crossed the river from east to west and back again, then he put it back on and it was dry."

Bikhit al-Bishari reproached himself. He feared the maleficent hand of the unknown: Yusuf Salim is a virtuous man. He used to do a good business. His shop was a room in his house that looked out onto the street. When the shaykh chose that particular room as the retreat in which to worship the One God, Yusuf Salim left off the butcher's trade and became the shaykh's deputy. The shaykh closes the door of his room during the day and fools think that he's still inside, when the good man is actually walking around blessed Mecca, home of the blameless Prophet's tomb. One pilgrimage year, Hajj Hasan Abdallah glimpsed the shaykh wedged between the crowds of pilgrims. He called out to him but that very instant the shaykh disappeared without a trace. True, the shaykh doesn't like to show off his piety. Until now, no one has ever seen him enter the mosque to pray, but he prays all right. On Friday in particular he prays in the Prophet's own mosque in Medina. Whoever says anything different is ignorant of the rank and consequence of the Lord's saints.

Were it not for the illness that confines him, Bikhit would visit the shaykh and kiss his hand and weep at his feet. He would take his place amongst the shaykh's disciples and companions. He would listen to them talk and they would listen to him. He would smoke sweet tobacco and inhale the odor of incense wafting from some distant unknown place. He would join the ritual chants and eat bone-building meat.

A Letter

Three and a half months after the arrival of Abd al-Hakam's letter to his family, a letter from Mustafa to his family arrived at Shaykh Fadil's address.

Mustafa informed his father, al-Bishari, of the dispute that had arisen between him and foreman Abd al-Dahir, and he begged his father not to interfere, nor to question him further on a settled matter. Mustafa said, "I'm a man who knows his own best interests. Don't worry about me. I've written to foreman Said Aqil in Palestine. I sent the letter by express mail. A whole week has passed since I sent it. As soon as foreman Said replies, I'll set off for Palestine. Greetings to my beloved mother Hazina and to my beloved sister Fahima (who I hope will find peace and protection under the roof of a good man. May he yet knock on your door, and may the wedding be celebrated in your lifetime my father, which I pray God to preserve and extend)."

The Beloved's Perfume

Shaykh Fadil finished reading the letter out loud and began to fold it. Hazina snatched it from his hands. She smelled it and kissed it, and Fahima did the same. Bikhit al-Bishari could not hide his joy at his son's letter either. He asked for it, and he smelled it and kissed it, and caught back the tears that sprang to his eyes so as not to look like a weakling. He was still, after all, the master of the house.

The Mysterious Scribe

Everyone was so happy with the absent son's letter that they forgot to ask Shaykh Fadil who had written it for the illiterate Mustafa. Shaykh Fadil was the only one who had seen the sentence scrawled on the back of the envelope: "With greetings from Muhammad Ahmad, this letter's scribe. And greetings to the postman too."

Shaykh Fadil wondered, "Who are you Muhammad Ahmad, and from which country?"

The Virgin's Heart in the Box

A

Suddenly, the girl loses interest in conversation because of the heavy weight pressing down on her chest. She stares, from a height, at the chest riven in two, and sees two breasts like shining suns. Thus her dialogue with her own heart swells:

My groom is coming on his horse. My groom is mounted in his saddle. My groom knocks on our door and it's I who will open the door. If not today, then tomorrow, if not today, then tomorrow, and that's God's will. I'll rejoice if he comes rich but if he comes poor, that's my lot. The rich girl for the rich man and the poor girl for the poor man. But I'm pretty—do you think I'm pretty, rich man? Everything your heart desires I possess, my husband. Here are my beautiful things in this wooden box adorned with pictures of the epic heroes al-Zinati Khalifa, al-Hilali Salama, Kulayb, Jassas and wailing Basus: a kohl jar, fringed kerchiefs in many colors, a flask of perfume, a patterned dress, a bar of scented soap.

B

Fahima opened her wooden box and took out Mustafa's letter from in between the folds of the patterned dress. She smelled it and kissed it, ever hungry, ever thirsty.

Her eyes wandered between the picture on the stamp and the picture on the box, and she said to herself, in discussion with herself: This is the king of Egypt and Sudan with a curled mustache, a red fez, and gold medals on his chest and shoulders. And this is al-Zinati Khalifa, felled by the hand of al-Hilali Salama, and he's got a curled mustache even bigger than the king's! And this is al-Hilali, slayer of al-Zinati, with not a single medal on his chest and shoulders. Mustafa had no mustache on the day he left home. Does he have one now to curl?

From the Levant

Four months after the arrival of Mustafa's first letter from the Sudan, his second letter arrived from the Levant. In it was a postal money order. Mustafa said, "I am well, and Palestine is God's paradise on earth. Nothing worries me but the distance of my kith and kin."

Another Letter from the Levant

Barely two more months had passed before another letter arrived from Mustafa. This one had less money in it than the first. Mustafa said, "I am well but bitter is the loneliness of the stranger cut off from his people."

Shaykh Fadil's Dialogue with Himself

Shaykh Fadil took his leave of Bikhit al-Bishari, passed five low-walled mud houses, then said to himself (he, the one who had read out both letters), "Two pounds, then one, then fifty piasters? Then comes nothing. That's how sons step into the world and learn something about it. Money in the hands of youth means corruption, and in the hands of a poor boy like Mustafa, it's twice as bad."

Shaykh Fadil remembered the following details and smiled:

1. There is a new bed in Bikhit al-Bishari's house. Its green palm leaves haven't even dried yet.

2. Hazina ordered Fahima to bring a mat and spread it on the stone bench for him to sit down on. The mat was new and made of bamboo.

3. Fahima brought a glass of tea on a new tray. The tray was painted with big red roses nestled in a profusion of tiny green leaves.

Chapter Two

I: What Man Fears

A

Bikhit al-Bishari lay stretched out on the bed of palm leaves made with his own hands before disease struck him two years ago. Hazina uncovered his face. There, she saw three colors — black, blue, and yellow — and she divined the approach of death. She said to Fahima, "Run girl, and don't come back without Shaykh Fadil," and as she watched the covers rise and fall over the chest, she thought to herself, "He fights with the determination of a man."

B

Shaykh Fadil drew up the hem of his white silk cloak and prepared to sit down. Hazina swore on the Prophet — most noble of God's creatures, peace and blessings upon him — that Shaykh Fadil must on no account dirty his clean clothes by sitting on the naked bench. Fahima scurried off and returned with a mat that she spread on the bench. Shaykh Fadil sat down.

C

The wind buffets the large, brittle leaves of the doum tree. They rub against each other and produce a sound like that of snakes slithering through grassy undergrowth. The soft, golden evening sunlight washes the earth and walls of the narrow yard.

Shaykh Fadil pointed out the benefits of the sun's golden rays for the sick man. Hazina, sitting on the ground next to her husband's bed, kept her silence. Fahima, sitting on the ground next to her mother, kept her silence. She thought, "I'll be guided by my mother in everything she does. I haven't yet learned what she has learned."

Shaykh Fadil turned Bikhit al-Bishari's head in the direction of blessed Mecca. He parted the lips and poured pure water between them. He bent over his ear and declared, "There is no God but the One God and Sayyidna Muhammad is His prophet." Shaykh Fadil went back and sat down on the mat on the stone bench.

Heavy darkness suddenly fell on the yard. Shaykh Fadil divined through long experience that the Angel of Death had arrived, and shrewd Hazina confirmed it, "Yes, it's the Angel of Death." In her ignorance, Fahima supposed that the sun had set, there, behind the western hills, but she closed her eyes—like her mother and Shaykh Fadil—to protect them, for the dust was flying in all directions from the beating of the two large wings.

Hazina heard and Fahima heard and Shaykh Fadil heard the door close behind the Angel of Death with the soul of Bikhit al-Bishari in his arms. The girl was unable to stifle a loud cry, but the experienced mother held back her wails and unleashed her tears instead. She knows that there are duties toward the dead that must be fulfilled before embarking on the period of mourning. Shaykh Fadil murmured, "We belong to God and to Him we shall return."

D

The mourning women wail and slap their cheeks alongside Hazina—not out of love for Bikhit in his lifetime, nor from anguish over his death, as Hazina well knows. She knows that every one of them is calling out to her own beloved ghosts. Her mind meanwhile is far away, with the distant boy who will not attend his father's funeral, with the deceased husband, with the men in the next room.

They remove the hair from the armpits and the pubis. They wash the body with water, and they rub it down with bitter herbs. They send for the white shrouds. They carry him out on a wooden platform and pray over his body. They lower the body into the pit, then they toss earth over it. And she must find the money for the chanters who will come to recite the Qur'an over his soul and beg for forgiveness and mercy.

II: The Living Have Obligations to the Family of the Deceased

A

Shaykh Fadil performed his sacred duties to the people of the house. He led the congregation in prayer; he paid for the white shrouds from his own pocket and for the chanter who recited the Qur'an over Bikhit al-Bishari's soul to beg for forgiveness and mercy.

The days of mourning passed in what seemed like the blink of an eye. Bikhit al-Bishari has departed the land of the living. Fahima sits opposite Hazina, Hazina sits opposite Fahima. Their breadwinner is in faraway foreign lands. And here they are, the girl and her mother, confronting the world alone.

The women paying condolences had bustled about the house all throughout the mourning period. They brought tea from their homes for Hazina and Fahima's breakfast and eggs and cheese for Hazina and Fahima's lunch. Their dinner usually consisted of fried meat and stewed vegetables. After breakfast and after lunch but before sunset, the women improvised dirges in grief-stricken, heart-wrenching voices.

Fahima learned to repeat the women's dirges under her breath so that in time, she could take her aging mother's place and discharge this duty at the funerals of all those who had come to mourn her father.

The wedding party, I wish I'd seen it,
I broke the pen and the ink I dried it
The wedding party, I wish I'd spied it,
I broke the pen and the ink I spilled it.

B

Shaykh Fadil brandished the wooden sword in the men's faces from atop the pulpit of his grandfather Abdallah's mosque, and he preached to the congregation: "You must stop your women from repeating these dirges. Men are the masters of women, and God will never have mercy on you if you don't order your women to refrain from such sin. These are pagan customs and you are Muslims! Expose not your dead and yourselves to God's grievous punishment. Pray over the souls of the dead and God will forgive them, and you, and us all. Verily, God is all-forgiving and all-merciful."

C

Shaykh Fadil sent a letter to the address of Foreman Said in Palestine and asked him to give it to Mustafa Bikhit immediately. Shaykh Fadil wrote in the letter, "Your father Bikhit al-Bishari has moved from the House of Transience to the House of Eternity. Adorn yourself with patience, my son, for there is no place in our religion for those who slap their cheeks, tear their clothes, and invoke the chants of the Time of Ignorance. We are all destined to annihilation. God alone is abiding."

Mustafa's letter arrived quickly. He said, "I don't believe it and I refuse to believe it. My father is alive, but far away, as you all are far away. This is God's will. I wish I could have seen him before he departed! I send you money for the funeral expenses. God alone is abiding. May you have long lives. We belong to God and to Him we shall return."

III: The River of Life Flows On

A

Hazina dictated to Shaykh Fadil. He wrote, "Al-Haddad al-Jabali has asked for your sister Fahima's hand. We've postponed our answer until you send your consent." On his own account he added, "Al-Haddad has a good reputation and is easy to get along with. He inherited a house from his father. His only dependent is his sister al-Haddada, wife of the deceased Qinawi Dahi, and I needn't remind you that Dahi was a smart man and left her a nest egg of her own. May God bless his soul and guide us all on the straight and true path."

Shaykh Fadil concluded the letter with a postscript in which he charged Mustafa to take care of his mother and to respect all possessors of wombs. He reminded him of the Prophet's saying, "Paradise is trodden by the feet of mothers." Hazina grasped Shaykh Fadil's hand and kissed it, and Fahima did the same.

Hazina and Fahima accompanied Shaykh Fadil to the door. Hazina took off her headscarf, shook out her white hair, raised her arms heavenward and gazed at the wide-open blue sky. She called on God: "O God, may wisdom and sagacity always be his companions, may his successors be blessed, and may he live a long life. The man stood by my daughter and me in our hardship."

B

Mustafa consented to his sister's marriage to al-Haddad. He sent money to help with the wedding expenses of the dear one, daughter of the mother and of the father, and he wrote, "If I could have sent more than this I would have—God only knows." He promised his mother a regular monthly sum, "to help with the necessities of this cruel life."

Hazina's face lit up with joy and she prayed for long life for Mustafa. When Shaykh Fadil folded Mustafa's letter, he noticed a postscript on the back of the paper. He read, "Bread and salt have bound me to a Levantine family. They have a beautiful and judicious daughter. My marriage may take place very soon."

C

The morning sun is bright and clear, and the truth—like the sun—is also clear, without a spot of ambiguity. When Hazina heard the news of her son's imminent marriage, black anger covered her face. Shaykh Fadil saw the black anger descend on Hazina's face, for she was incapable of concealing it. Such is the way of the world: until the tempest comes to sweep mankind off the face of the earth, the son's mother will always be jealous of the son's wife.

Chapter Three

From Palestine, the promised sum reached Hazina regularly. It was interrupted just once, and Mustafa apologized the following month: "Our beloved wife miscarried in her fourth month, but now she is in good health. If not for this compelling reason, we would have never been late in sending the usual sum."

Fahima went often to her mother's house on the pretext of paying a visit. How to digest these repeated visits from a newlywed? And did it escape Hazina that al-Haddad would also come immediately on Fahima's heels, as though he were a piece of straw caught in the hem of her dress?

"Hmph! What's al-Haddad afraid of?" Ah, that the girl will confide a secret to her mother, a secret that al-Haddad does not want Hazina to know.

Each time Fahima came, al-Haddad came after her. He would stay exactly the amount of time it takes to drink a glass of tea, then get up and throw a reproachful glance at Fahima. The girl would rise and follow her husband in silence, and they never exchanged a single word, nor did they speak to Hazina.

The old woman martialed her arts and created an opportunity to be alone with her daughter. "Don't be shy. Confide in me, daughter—I'm your mother." Maneuvering, she added, "A man tills his land, plows it, seeds it, and waters it without cease, then he reaps the harvest. Does al-Haddad till his land? Or is the land ungrateful and miserly? Speak!"

Fahima hesitated. "First he blows out the lamp and comes to bed. He gathers me up in his arms and strains and struggles wildly, but some force holds him back. A long time passes before he finally calms down. Then he cries like a baby."

Hazina chided Fahima and accused her of great stupidity and feeble-mindedness. She warned her not to breathe a word of what she had just told her to a living soul, and she added reproachfully, "You kept this from your mother all this time? Such things should never be ignored. It's not as big a problem as you think: Another woman wants to take al-Haddad away from you, Fahima, and the wretched woman has gotten the help of a powerful daughter of the jinn. Thus was the evil deed perpetrated. Shaykh Alimi who lives in a hamlet in the western hills can send the evil right back to its owner. With his capable hands he'll untie the ropes that bind al-Haddad's manhood."

Hazina went to see Shaykh Alimi. She knocked on the door of his solitude in the hamlet in the western hills. He answered the knock and listened to her complaint, and he gave her the heart of a white hoopoe and a small flask of murky liquid and a piece of paper folded ninety-nine times. Hazina offered him two brass coins in the palm of her outstretched hand. The honest shaykh refused at first but finally accepted at Hazina's insistent pleas.

When the cocks crowed from the rooftops, Hazina got out of bed and put on her cloak. She avoided meeting any women in order to preserve the paper's efficacy. Underneath al-Haddad's doorstep, she buried the paper of ninety-nine folds. As for the white hoopoe's heart, it must be roasted and pound into a fine meal. The meal must be scattered behind every visitor who sets foot across the threshold of al-Haddad's house.

"Careful, Fahima my daughter. If al-Haddad steps on the meal, all is lost!"

"I won't tell my daughter the secret of this murky liquid, this semen from the loins of a potent jinn. Fahima must place a single drop—no more—into a pot of pure water. Al-Haddad bathes in it and Fahima keeps the water. The next day, Fahima repeats the procedure using two drops instead of one. Al-Haddad bathes and Fahima keeps the water. The procedure must be repeated for six days, not including the blessed Friday. The drops increase with the number of days. It must be so, or all will be lost. Before sunrise on the seventh day, Fahima must bathe in the water that she has collected over the past six days, after which she must go to her husband's bed. All shall then be well with God's permission and she shall have her wish from the Lord of Mankind."

Mustafa apologized for not sending larger sums of money (the estrangement between Fahima and al-Haddad is costly). The inexperienced girl doesn't carry out the instructions properly and ruins everything. Al-Haddad now steers clear of Hazina, even when she visits him in his own house. He avoids her eyes and comes up with all sorts of implausible excuses in order to get away, as though Hazina were a devil. The girl confides in her mother that al-Haddad beats her and only comes home to sleep after long nights spent in town with loafers and scoundrels.

"He smokes hashish at Tawfiq al-Siq's place, Mother. He sucks on opium and keeps stashes of it in his pockets. He hides his impotence by chasing other men's women. Al-Haddada, his sister, throws false accusations at me. She says that I take my husband's business into my mother's house."

"Al-Haddada has lit a fire with which to burn my daughter," Hazina thought.

"Can you believe it, Mother? He has openly accused me of being barren!"

Al-Haddad will divorce Fahima. If not today, then tomorrow or in a month or a year at most. The divorce is coming, no doubt about it, and al-Haddada, the sister, is preparing the way by spreading the word that Hazina's daughter is barren. When al-Haddad divorces Fahima, no other suitor will come forward. The girl will stay with Hazina in al-Bishari's house, defective goods, a barren spinster, a sullied doorstep. Al-Haddada covets her brother's land. She wants al-Haddad to remain childless so that she and her own children from Qinawi Dahi can inherit it.

This then is how matters stand. A speedy way around the prohibition must be found. Al-Haddad's perpetually drugged mind will never see through the stitches of Hazina's needle.

The old woman said to the girl, "Maybe the fault is yours."

"He hasn't touched me," the girl replied.

The mother said, "We'll try—just to make sure."

Here is the ancient massive-stoned temple, ruined by impudent time. The seven gates of the temple are still intact, however. Above every gate sits a winged sun disk guarded by two interlaced snakes.

There, inside, is the hall of columns where the people of old used to offer their prayers. In this hall they burned piles of incense brought from the farthest reaches of the civilized world. Inside, trapped in his narrow chamber, lurks the naked-loined god of procreation. The unfinished obelisk— the sonorous obelisk—and the sacred pond lie beyond. Its waters neither rise nor fall in spite of the springs that weep ceaselessly into its small basin. The earth's treasures lie here under the water: necklaces and bracelets that clasped the necks and wrists of thousands of kings and queens.

In front of the gate of the ancient temple, Hazina stood talking to Urabi Abu Fikri. Her eyes roamed over the rams: These rams were human beings in ancient times but God's wrath transformed the people of old into stone, as punishment for their unbelief. True . . . how can a brother marry his sister? A son, his mother? Here are the sinful folk ranged in twin rows with the heads of rams and the bodies of lions.

Urabi Abu Fikri approached Fahima and said, "Follow me."

Fahima will come face-to-face with the man who boasted of his manhood, so that God turned him into cold black stone, his genitals exposed for all eternity: "They left him with the women and went off to war, a war that lasted for many long years. He sent them sons for their armies and when victory was finally theirs, they set him up as a god to the exclusion of the One and Only."

The key screeched in the rusty lock and the enormous iron gate creaked open. Urabi Abu Fikri said to Fahima, "Go inside," so she went inside and Urabi closed the gate behind her.

Fahima is alone now, and the chamber is damp and musty. Bats fly close to her face and disturb the still air. Fahima can hear the sound of her breath and of her beating heart. Slowly, by the faint rays descending from a skylight high up in the ceiling, her eyes make out the silhouette of the naked black giant, and she sees two red eyes glowing like coals. She tries to scream but the scream sticks in her throat. She tries to still the sudden violent shaking of her body as she watches the naked black giant move closer.

Thickly falls the darkness: vision sputters and fails. Heart misses its beats, mind spins delirious, but her ear continues to pick out the thump of heavy stone feet on the stone floor.

Fahima fell backward into outstretched arms and lost consciousness.

This is my mother's house. I am lying on my dead father's bed. The person standing over there is my mother. She's taking care of me. She cools my burning forehead and smoothes my burning face. She rubs my neck and chest. The cool water is good, and the warm water is good, and the long sleep that approaches is good. I crave moist dates.... But why are the days passing so quickly? I smell the smell of his sweat. I smell the smell of urine on the dry earth, and of rotten green sycamore fruit. I crave it. You're my brother and I'm the daughter of the mother and the father. Here are my arms. Take me. Come.

Fahima drank warm tea and fell into a deep sleep.

Chapter Four

The Cunning One

He is the Great Contriver. He sent death to Umar Ibn al-Khattab in the shape of a dagger clasped in the hand of a vile Magian. He is the Prince of Believers. He is the One who scattered the seed in Fahima's belly and behold: she is with child after a year and a half of marriage to al-Haddad.

Hazina schemed, but God is the Most Excellent Schemer, and now Hazina harvests the bitter fruit. Fahima has left al-Haddad's house thrice divorced and al-Haddad will take no pity on her swollen belly.

A Letter to Mustafa and a Letter from Mustafa

Shaykh Fadil summed up the abominable news as follows: "That which both God and man detest has come to pass. Your sister Fahima has been divorced without recourse."

Hazina waited patiently for the reply, fighting off the devil's whispers by day and the terrible visions of dreams by night. She feared above all that black suspicion would kill her son in faraway foreign lands. But Mustafa's reply to Shaykh Fadil's letter arrived. It contained money and instructions: "Half the money is for Fahima's expected child. If it's a boy, call him al-Bishari."

To the Market

On the first Tuesday after the arrival of the money Mustafa had sent, Hazina went to the market in town and bought two large rabbits, a black male and a white female.

"The female is pregnant, God willing, and Fahima must have meat to eat when she delivers. Four bunches of carrots, the sweet orange fruit for her and the green leaves for the rabbits, and chewing gum, to help her pass the endless hours now that she's been forbidden to move about till her time. Fahima craves purple grapes but it's not the season. How strange pregnant women's cravings are."

The Road Home is Long

Before she was halfway home Hazina felt tired so she sat down to rest in the sparse shade of an acacia tree. She kept her one good eye trained on the road to catch some daughter of Adam heading back from the market, because the road is long and requires a companion.

Good fortune arrived in the form of Amina, al-Tahami's wife—a woman who keeps herself to herself and holds her tongue thanks to her many children and the cares of life. Hazina told Amina about pregnant Fahima's craving for purple grapes out of season. Amina said the baby would be born with a birthmark in the form of a grape if her wish wasn't satisfied. She laughed and added, "And maybe even a whole cluster of fat, swollen grapes!" Hazina laughed too and remarked, "Girls today are spoiled. I didn't want anything when I was pregnant with Mustafa or Fahima."

In order to have a bit of fun and to shorten the trip, and to avoid the subject of Fahima's divorce and to expel the image of a legless beggar she had seen in the marketplace,

Amina replied, "You should thank God. Better grapes than watermelon."

They shared a short, amputated laugh after which neither of them could think of anything else to say until they reached the entrance to the village. Under the Christ's-thorn tree that goes by the name of 'God's Tree' and next to the clay jar brimming with water for the thirsty traveler, they promised to call on each other soon and then they parted ways, each to her own house.

Chapter Five

Why Nabawiya?

Al-Haddad visited his former wife in order to see the baby girl. He slipped two coins in the child's swaddling clothes and avoided Fahima with his eyes. "I came for my daughter's sake," he warned Hazina. "The money is for her."

He objected to naming her Nabawiya. "Why Nabawiya?" he demanded. "There are lots of beautiful names. Why do you refuse the nice ones? Hmph. They don't cost anything! I'm going to call her Houriya. That's a lovely name, and the girl is lovely—can't you see?"

A Second Visit

Al-Haddad brought his daughter some colored calico, "Because winter is on the way." It annoyed him that Hazina and Fahima insisted on calling his lovely daughter Houriya, Nabawiya. He decided not to bother discussing it with them again. He would just keep calling her Houriya. "When Hazina makes up her mind the whole universe can't change it and Fahima is her mother's daughter." Al-Haddad chided himself for even thinking about taking Fahima back. "I would have maybe done it for Houriya's sake," he ruefully thought.

He prayed God to protect him from that wily old woman called Hazina. "She made me go to court for the first time in my life, and stand before a judge who ordered me to pay alimony and the divorce settlement. Hazina won't leave me alone until I agree to pay child support for the little one. I won't go back to court. We'll come to some sort of agreement, but I'll never take Hazina's daughter back. She wound suspicion round my manhood and surrounded me with gloating eyes."

The Decision

"I'll pay one and a half riyals to my daughter Houriya. I'll send the money with a third party. Houriya will grow up and I'll get her back from Fahima by order of the courts. This is my final decision. Better safe than sorry."

And to put the matter to rest once and for all, al-Haddad decided to approach his sister about arranging a marriage for him with the fisherman's daughter.

Chapter Six

It All Happened So Unexpectedly

A

Abd al-Hakam Taha came from Palestine. He brought gifts
from Mustafa: a small crate of hazelnuts and dried figs and
apricots, a black gown for the mother and a patterned gown
for the sister. There was a black headscarf for each, and for
the little girl Nabawiya a length of cloth large enough for
three dresses, yellow shoes with red buckles, and a small
candy bull with two pointy horns.

Hazina distributed some of the gifts to the neighbors.
"Didn't they stand by me during the worst of those evil days?
They did their duty and now I'm doing mine."

Two gold teeth shone when Abd al-Hakam, son of
Tafida, laughed out loud. He said, "Mustafa is in excellent
health. He misses his mother and his sister and he longs
to see the little one, Nabawiya. We work with the British
army under foreman Ahmad al-Zinbai. Ahmad al-Zinbai is
a countryman from the west bank of Luxor. He asked me
to visit his family and deliver some things. I'll visit them
today. We might be coming home soon. Mustafa divorced
his Levantine wife. She was barren. Mustafa gave me some
money for you."

Abd al-Hakam took out his wallet—it was of yellow leather, swollen, with a green sphinx's head stamped on it—and plucked a pound note from a bankroll tied with a rubber band. He offered the note to Hazina. Hazina took it, smiling.

"He's divorced his wife . . . he'll stay mine in heart and wealth. I'm the one who carried him in my belly for nine months and put up with his filth when he was nothing but a mass of shitting, screaming flesh. Abd al-Hakam will think I'm smiling because of the money. Abd al-Hakam's got lots of money. I wish Mustafa would come home. . . . The English must be swimming in loot. They've discovered the treasures of King Qarun, and they're using them to pay their workers."

Abd al-Hakam said, "I'm very busy and this is my second visit to you. Time is short. Today I'm going to visit my mother's family in Multaqa. I've got all sorts of letters and gifts from my friends and colleagues and I have to contact their families. I'll visit you again soon—before leaving, God willing. Goodbye," and he glanced at Fahima and smiled. He opened his mouth and closed it again over the shining gold. "Maybe you'd like to send something to Mustafa?"

Fahima said, "Come have lunch with us. I'll slaughter a pigeon for you." Abd al-Hakam smiled, proud of his two gold teeth. Fahima smiled back shyly.

"You're our guest," Hazina insisted. "You're exactly like Mustafa. I should have priority over everyone else."

"I'll do my best," Abd al-Hakam replied and he thanked Fahima and Hazina for their kindness. He invited them to be his guests at his parents' house where they would be made more than welcome, and he smiled again.

"Did he just wink at me?" Fahima wondered.

He pressed her hand and kept it in his for a moment, and his gold teeth shone. This time, she was sure he had winked.

Is he looking to get married, or has people's gossip made him greedy? With the money he has he could marry a well-born girl, and much prettier than Fahima. But the heart has its own ways and a man in love might even consider marrying a divorced woman. Why not? Fahima still hasn't lost her freshness, nor her looks, and men still desire her.

Hazina and Fahima visited Abd al-Hakam at his parents' house. They agreed that Fahima would meet him at the railroad station with the things for Mustafa. "I'm taking the dawn train," said Abd al-Hakam. "I'll wait for you in front of the station, so don't buy an entrance ticket."

Hazina said, "Nabawiya, Fahima's daughter, is already walking and talking as you can see," and she turned to Nabawiya. "Say something, precious. Tell your uncle Abd al-Hakam to say hello to your uncle Mustafa."

The girl Nabawiya repeated her grandmother's words. "Say hello to my uncle Mustafa, Uncle Abd al-Hakam."

This annoyed Fahima. "She's only reminding him that I was married and divorced and have a daughter to feed on top of it all."

Neither Hazina nor Fahima slept that night. Even Nabawiya stayed up late, rummaging around, chasing moonbeams and the rays of the dim lamp, laughing at the top of her lungs. They made the round loaves from fine white flour. They brushed them with butter and sprinkled them with sugar, and the hot oven didn't burn a single loaf.

The dawn call to prayer has not yet rung out. The basket is full of loaves and dates and the cover is secured with hemp cord. The time draws near. Fahima gets moving. She sets off for the railroad station in town. Abd al-Hakam meets her at the entrance. He takes the basket off her head and gazes at her face. She lowers her eyes shyly. His descending hand brushes against her breast, and the breast trembles.

"Deliberate or not, there was a promise in his farewell, in the heat that traveled from his palm to mine."

The road back is long. Going was shorter.

Dawn lifts the shadows from the houses and sweeps them away. They collect over there, on the distant horizon. The sun has not yet risen, even though this is its light.

Suddenly, a mad scream rings out, rising and ripping through the silence.

When Fahima reached home Hazina said, "Al-Haddad and the fisherman's daughter have been burnt alive."

Night and stifling heat. Sleep-desire won't come. Her mind spins in the vortex of delirious thoughts. Fahima cannot stop chasing after the images.

"The fisherman's daughter is fair-skinned, like a duck in flesh and fat. Her eyes are wide and black, even without kohl. Her long eyelashes shine like her long black hair. If the fisherman's daughter uncovers her bosom, al-Haddad will see two pointing breasts—the white flesh, the dark nipple, the cleft. Al-Haddad will start up. He'll strain and struggle wildly, he'll clasp the body tight, he'll fear the coming scandal. He'll bite and tear the flesh and silence the scream by sprinkling them both with kerosene and setting it all aflame. He'll burn to death and so will his secret. . . .

"I knew his secret too. Maybe he would have burned me alive as well if he could have. Will I ever have peace of mind again after today? I don't think so."

B

This war has got nothing to do with us. Nonetheless, the authorities draft our children into the army and force them to work in the camps of the cursed English Redskins. Those who can afford it pay the bribe and the poor man begs his son to cut off his trigger finger.

Some goods disappeared and others rotted. The price of everything shot up. Things which cost a milleme now cost a penny. Powdered, cubed, and rock sugar vanished. Tea was sweetened with pieces of candy and sugared almonds. Kerosene and oil grew scarce. Candles and lamps were lit with twine dipped in animal fat. Some people grew rich while most grew even poorer and theft became commonplace. No letters were sent to sons and none arrived. May this fire consume the English and Hitler and the grocers and the king and the shroud dealers!

Chapter Seven

A

Disabled Hassan recited the opening sura of the Qur'an and finished with a quick reading of Chapter One, The Cow. He asked Hazina and Fahima to pray over the souls of those who died in God and his Prophet's faith. He rose from his seat and unfurled the sleeve that covered his amputated right hand. Hazina emptied the dates and yellow bread baked with milk and turmeric from her small basket and into Hassan's sleeve. Hassan left to recite over another nearby grave where a group of women were sitting and waiting.

Hazina pointed to the women and said to Fahima, "The men's womenfolk—the men who died in the antiquities accident on the west bank." Fahima shuddered. Her mother was talking about the old accident and the old temple, with the hall and the dark chamber and the naked black man.

"I'll fight it," Fahima said to herself. "I'll be stubborn."

Hazina feebly picked her way along the dusty, crooked paths surrounded by burial mounds frozen still in the shadows cast by the glowing, heatless sunset. Fahima followed her. The henna trees rustled in the breeze and showered them with yellow petals. They threaded their way carefully down the path, terrified of the consequences should they step on the bones of the dead.

The accident that befell the men who died in the old temple frightens Fahima but Hazina insists on retelling the old story:

"A man came out of the tunnel. His face was grimy and the sweat poured down his neck and formed chunks of black mud on his chest. The man talked to foreman Basyuni, who told the French antiquities inspector what the man said. The inspector jabbered something in French. He raised his short stick in the air and waved it around in foreman Basyuni and the grimy man's faces. 'The sons of Arabs play and don't work! The sons of Arabs don't like to work!' Foreman Basyuni shouted at the grimy man and the man immediately went back down into the tunnel to pass on the order to the other men. Then the earth groaned by its Lord's command and the world turned upside down. It happened at midday and the men's bodies were removed just before sunset."

With a woman's weakness Fahima struggled to expel the black visions, but her mind disobeyed. She gave in to the all-powerful force compelling her to follow her mother's steps.

She said to herself, "Think about what happened to the men in the temple, don't think about what happened to you there. Don't give in or you'll find yourself in the naked black god's chamber again. The French engineer's carriage fell into the Nile and he drowned. He was drunk and his wife was with him. Foreman Basyuni's wife keeps giving birth but the babies all die in their first month."

End of the story, "The Accident in the Temple." Fahima tried to think of another story to take her mind off what happened in the god's chamber. She remembered the story of the three jinns and said, "I'll tell it to myself."

Three widows, three sisters, covered from head to foot in long black veils. They appear at midday when the sun is at its zenith—a red eye burning bright as hell—and when the traveler's shadow is like a peg driven into the ground. The burial mounds open their maws and out spill tongues of fire. Three widows, three jinns. They lay their hands on the huge grindstone that never stops turning. It grinds stray dogs and cats to bits. Their bones break with a loud cracking noise and blood mixes with flesh. The blood jumps hotly from the flesh, spattering the faces of the three jinns. Their eyes spark, their faces ooze rich red lust, their lunatic laughter reaches the sky and shakes the earth. The all-powerful ones. The wolf-toothed.

Voices ring in Fahima's ears, dogs howling, cats screeching, frogs croaking, flesh crackling and grindstone grinding, a grindstone rhythmically, incessantly grinding, and to this regular, continuous beat the naked black man comes closer, his stone feet pounding on the stone floor.

B

Hazina woke to the sound of Fahima's screams. "Mother! Mother!"

She jumped out of bed in a panic.

Fahima said, "The cold . . . the cold, Mother."

True, the girl's body is shaking from head to foot and her face is on fire!

Hazina collected all the blankets in the house and piled them onto her body. She wet a cloth with water and vinegar and applied it to Fahima's forehead; she stayed by her side till morning. Terror struck her when she saw her daughter's face turn the three colors: yellow, black, and blue. "It's the death-fever," she said to herself.

The barber, Ma'mun al-Mudakallim, came to the house. He shaved Fahima's head, bled it with a razor and drew out the impure blood with a cupping glass. He filled five cupping glasses with dark, dirty blood and he said, "The impure blood corrupts the pure blood that will preserve Fahima's life." If her body could have withstood it, he would have drawn two more glasses to be sure of her recovery. Ma'mun the barber said he would come back to check on his patient directly after noon prayers.

He came back and found Fahima delirious as before, so he lit a fire and heated an iron nail and passed it over Fahima's head three times. Then he said, "This way I will have destroyed the cloudy, corrupt blood, after which it's all in God's hands. He alone is omnipotent."

Hope flared and sparked. One-eyed Yusuf gave the call to dusk prayers from atop Abdallah's mosque, then the call to sunset prayers, then evening prayers, and the inexperienced girl smiles.

Hazina screamed at the sight of the newcomer, and she split her gown in two. "No, no, it's not you she wants! It's just that she's young and can't bear the pain. It's not you she desires. She only wants the suffering to end and the body to find rest. She's a fool, and can't see that you are death."

Chapter Eight

Nabawiya is her father's legatee by right and law. Al-Haddad's sister—who hates Nabawiya and Nabawiya's mother and grandmother—planned and plotted how to defraud the little girl of her God-given rights. Al-Haddada said, "My brother— may God rest his soul—sold me his inheritance and here is the official deed, inked with al-Haddad's thumbprint." Hazina sought out Shaykh Fadil to protect her and to thwart al-Haddada's stratagems. Al-Haddada sought help from Shaykh Yusri, son of Yusuf Diyab. He had failed his studies at the blessed Azhar, but because he had spent two years living in the University Hostel for southerners he is now the master of the village school. The little ones memorize the Qur'an at his hands. He improvises joyful poems at weddings and recites them into the microphones. At funerals, he improvises mournful poems and recites them into the microphones.

Shaykh Yusri said to al-Haddada, "Leave it to me. Your job is to hurry up and register the deed at the Registry Office." And he offered to marry al-Haddada's daughter Inshirah.

Al-Haddada replied, "The girl is still young and you've already got three wives."

Shaykh Yusri said, "Four is my God-given right."

"Give me some time to think about it."

"To think about what?"

"My two other daughters' marriages cost me a lot of money and I can't afford a third wedding. I also have to seek al-Sa'di's advice. The boy has grown up and become a man. He's the one who will set his sister Inshirah's dowry."

Cunning al-Haddada smiles. "I'll get a big dowry from the old man. My daughter's dowry will be bigger than the dowries of his other wives. I said to the man, 'I'll seek advice from my son al-Sa'di.' Then I'll go back to him and say, 'Al-Sa'di refuses. Give me some time to convince him.' Then I'll go back and say to the old man, 'The boy wants a big dowry for his sister.' The old man will say, 'That's too much.' I'll tell him that I'll give him an answer in two days. 'I've agreed with al-Sa'di on so much. I tried my best, but he won't accept less than that.' The old man will accept because the girl is young and pretty and an heiress to boot."

Meanwhile, Shaykh Fadil said to Hazina, "We'll go to court. The judge will decide."

Chapter Nine

A Boy and a Girl

Shaykh Fadil owns an unenclosed date palm orchard behind his large house. Nabawiya ties each end of a long rope to the branch of a palm tree in order to make a swing. In between the two trees lies a vast space through which Nabawiya flies. She spreads out her arms and grasps the rope that cuts into her buttocks while the wind raises her dress and caresses her lovely face, blowing through her hair and bringing the joy that fashions laughter.

Shaykh Fadil's son (from deceased Asmaa) is close to Nabawiya in age. He is her only playmate. The boy has lots of pretty stories. He brings them back from school and tells them to Nabawiya. She listens and smiles, and sometimes laughs, and sometimes says to him, "You're talking nonsense!" He gets angry and she makes up with him and he tells her another story.

"Together with Luxor, this village of Karnak was in olden times the royal capital of Egypt and of the whole world. It used to be called Thebes back then. The temple was surrounded by a large wall, completely intact, with lots of gates. People prayed inside the temple and the townsfolk's houses all clustered around it. The tombs were on the west bank. The Road of Rams ran between the Karnak temple and the Luxor temple. The ancient Egyptians were not infidels as people now think.

They were the first to know God and they were the first to embalm the body using a secret method that neither men nor worms will ever discover, no matter how hard they try.

"The earth is a big ball spinning in space and in this space spin moons and suns and those stars you see up there in the sky. . . ."

Nabawiya laughed and repeated the boy's last words incredulously, "And those stars up there in the sky?"

He huffed and said, "You're just stupid."

Nabawiya realized that he was angry. "I'll make up with him," she said to herself. "Tell me the story of the king," she begged the motherless son. The boy reached back into the past. He remembered and he forgot his anger.

"The day before, the principal announced to the whole school at the morning assembly, 'Tomorrow each one of you comes to school washed and scrubbed and wearing his best clothes and his fez!' From Luxor Station all the way to the Karnak temple gates you could see people lined up on both sides of the road. Students and principals and teachers and village headmen and women and soldiers and officers, workers and employees from all the government offices cheering 'Long live Faruk, king of Egypt and the Sudan!' The carriage went by with the king inside. Its windows were open and it was pulled by eight horses white as milk. The curtains were also made of milky white silk but they were drawn so as to hide the king from the eyes of the public. . . ."

Nabawiya interrupted him. "He's got a glass eye!"

"Lies," the boy replied. "He's got a bright red face."

"You didn't see him," the girl retorted.

"Nobody saw him. But I've got a color picture of him in the encyclopedia. I've got the book and I'll show you the picture."

"They say he can eat a whole sheep all by himself," the girl continued.

"That's not true either," the boy emphatically replied. "The cook puts the sheep in a big pot with lots of water, then he puts the pot on the stove. The water slowly boils down till there's only a small glassful of liquid left and then the king drinks it."

The boy is beautiful in the girl's eyes. He is all boys. The boy is beautiful in the eyes of all the village girls, and for them too, he is all boys.

He wears a suit and he goes to the cinema in town every Thursday and sits in the balcony. He rides a bicycle and his soft hair flutters in the wind and falls into those clear, dark eyes ringed with natural kohl. His father owns a lot of land and orchards, horses and buffalo, donkeys and cattle and goats. His mother was a gentlewoman. Her grandfather is Yusuf Abd al-Karim Agha, her mother is Zannuba and her father is Abd al-Simih Abd al-Qadir.

Nabawiya's world is small—their house, the palm orchard, Shaykh Fadil's house, the river—but to her it is so vast. Even though her grandmother is old and irritable, constantly complaining, slow-moving, shortsighted, and near-deaf, she loves sweet things as much as Nabawiya does. Saliha—Shaykh Fadil's wife and sister of the deceased Asmaa—puts her to work: light the fire, put the coals in the brass crucible, buy the tobacco from the faraway shop, and change the dirty pipe water. But she is generous. She gives her a cucumber or a slice of watermelon or a handful of dates in return.

Nabawiya adores the river. The river fowl glide over the sun-tinted plane of the water and pluck out the dead fish floating on its surface. She loves to gaze at the boats with their billowing white sails, the high mountain and the yellow sands on the other bank. The houses look so small against the foot of the mountain, as though they were grazing goats.

Shaykh Fadil's son is fond of rabbits, big and small, black and white. It puzzles him how people can bear to skin those weak little creatures and grill them over coals or fry them in fat. Rabbits should never be eaten. They are too lovable.

Nabawiya lay in wait for the poor rabbit until it peeped out of its hole. She lay quite still and as soon as it had gone a bit further, she pounced down and laid hold of it. She held it up and said to the boy, "Look."

"It's dead," the boy said.

"Why can't I ever catch a live rabbit? They always die. All I want is to stroke its soft fur."

The boy closed his eyes and said, "Don't try to catch any more and then they won't die."

Nabawiya cried. She shivered and sobbed. She couldn't stop. But she held on fast to the dead rabbit.

Shaykh Fadil's son came closer. He stroked her back tenderly. He tried to soothe her. "Don't cry anymore."

Nabawiya's sobs only grew louder, so the boy gathered up her shaking body and pulled her close to his small chest. "Enough. Stop crying."

But Nabawiya wouldn't stop, and so Shaykh Fadil's son made himself think of his dead mother and burst out crying too.

Chapter Ten

I: Rumors and Entertaining Anecdotes
and True Events Too

A

The Cunning Jew with the hooked nose is selling three jugs of wine for less than a quarter of the going price. The rich Arab said to himself, "What a good bargain!" The Jew's lovely daughter dipped the tip of her tongue into a goblet full of wine and took a long, slow sip. She said, "Our wine is good." (The girl's hair is yellow, like molten gold, and each cheek is stamped with a red rose.)

The wine dripped over her mouth, into the cleft that marks the two breasts, and gathered in the navel.

The son of Arabs said, "That goblet is mine."

The daughter of Sarah said, "This goblet is yours."

The nose smells and the eye sees. The snake's skin is soft. The hair of the armpits and the pubis is long and flowing. Sweat has its odor and perfume has its odor. The dog yelps and the snake bites. The orchard is beautiful with its rows upon rows of orange trees. And the girl is lovely (on each cheek a red apple is stamped and her hair is more golden than a ripe orange). The days pass, as they must, and the rows of grapevines are as long as a lifetime and as wide as a lifetime.

B

The Jew—the new owner of the orchard—wants to dig a well to irrigate his trees. The sons of Arabs dug the well with their strong arms and the water gushed forth. The Greedy Jew said, "I'll pay you for your labor once you've dug a hole as deep as your height." The sons of Arabs did as he asked and the Jew flung the dirt onto the men and buried them alive. He said, "That's exactly the depth I wanted for my well."

II

The Zionist gangs massacred the sons and daughters of Arabs and the English departed from Palestine and gave it to the Jews in fulfillment of an old promise. The armies of the Arabs were shattered by treachery and defective arms. But God's troth is true and He never breaks his covenant. Children grow up—even in refugee camps. The rabbits multiplied and grew numerous in the house of the deceased Bikhit al-Bishari (from a black male and a white female bought by Hazina one long-ago day in the town market), and Nabawiya the orphan shed the enchanted collar of childhood. She looks at the red candy bull (she never did eat it; still keeps it, even though one of its pointing horns has broken off) and thinks of her dear uncle in Palestine.

III

After the catastrophe of the Nakba, the men returned from Palestine. They are right here in Egypt now, working in the British camps in the Canal Zone. The men earn their bread with their bare arms and pine for their families. The longing in their breasts is like God's eternal flame, but at least they're back in their own country and no matter how long it takes they'll come home one day to marry their cousins and people the land with their children.

IV

Mustafa commands all forty of the men: chosen men, strong and sturdy, obedient to him in everything, cunning as foxes, agile as cats, brave as Ibn al-Walid, resourceful as Mu'awiya, talented as Eve at trickery and card games.

One of them chooses a victim inside the British camp—an Australian, an Indian, or an African. They tempt him with cards. Gambling is risky business and alcohol is gambling's best friend. Alcohol intoxicates the brain and ignites the lust for plunder. Date-palm wine is an Egyptian invention—strong and quick in effect. Mustafa had brought a bottle containing a magic potion with him from the Sudan, land of heat and amulets and holy saints. He bought it from a powerful wizard back in the days when he used to work there. One drop of this liquid in a barrel of wine sends anyone who drinks a single glass into the deep sleep of Ephesius.

And everyone slept.

The camp suddenly has no guards. No one to see, no one to hear or fire a shot. Mustafa enters the camp at the head of his men, and the men gather up all the white feta cheese and the yellow Romano cheese, the jam, tea, butter, and bolts of warm woolen cloth. They fill up their baskets and carry them out on bent backs.

Once, Mustafa killed a high-ranking British officer.

The even higher-ranking British officer screams at the soldiers and his voice rings out in the camp: "Egyptians: crafty and rubbish!"

Mustafa's warehouses are underground. Nobody knows exactly where, except himself and his men. Even the jinn would never be able to find them. Mustafa's warehouses hold a priceless treasure.

V

A

Egypt's sons of all confession took up arms—even the men from the regime's military units. Demonstrations spilled out all across the Valley and the Egyptian government called for a boycott of the British invaders. Anyone dealing with the English is a traitor to the nation, and the government will provide jobs for all its native sons.

B

Shaykh Fadil subscribes to *The Egyptian*, the Wafd Party newspaper. He also subscribes to *Pulpit of the East*, the National Party newspaper run by Ali al-Ghayati, author of a patriotic volume of poetry and friend of Muhammad Farid (both of whom were put behind bars by the British).

C

Muhammad Ahmad al-Sharqawi—correspondent for *The Bloc* and *The Valley*—shouted at his children and the mother of his children. "Won't you stop screaming, you devils!"

Muhammad Ahmad al-Sharaqawi had just come back from the house of Amin Effendi Abd al-Sami', the brother of Saliha, Shaykh Fadil's sister. They had been listening to an Umm Kulthum record on Amin Effendi's gramophone. These were the words she sang: "Egypt in my heart and on my lips—I love her with all my soul and blood. / Who amongst you loves her so, who would sacrifice all for her sake?"

Muhammad Ahmad al-Sharqawi went into his room and closed the door behind him. He decided to write an article titled, "The Sea of the Past Flows into the Sea of the Present but the Sea is Not Yet Full." He would send the article by post to the *The Valley*. If *The Valley* failed to publish it within the week he would send it to *The Bloc*. And he will sign the article, "The Seasoned Reporter."

Muhammad Ahmad al-Sharqawi said to himself, "First I'll gather my thoughts together. I'll jot down some exemplary verses and some popular sayings and then I'll start writing my article tonight after everyone has gone to bed." And in an elegant Kufic hand he noted the following:

"The Sea of the Past Flows into the Sea of the Present but the Sea is Not Yet Full."

1. "My country, my country/ To you my love and fealty." An anthem sung by Sayyid Darwish for the revolution of 1919. Suitable for all voices and insurrections. Wonderful when sung in chorus. Why, I wonder?

2. "If I were not an Egyptian, I would ardently desire to be an Egyptian." Mustafa Kamil was a lawyer who adored French culture, and Turkish blood ran in his veins—but he was born in Egypt, grew up in Egypt, and drank of her Nile's waters.

3. "Our mothers bore us free men." The retort of Umar Ibn al-Khattab, prince of the Muslims, to Amr Ibn al-'As, governor of Egypt, when the latter's son attacked a Christian then arrogantly declared, "I am the son of a Muslim!" Urabi borrowed Ibn al-Khattab's phrase

and spat it out in the king's face while daring to remain mounted.

4. "If immortal fame should distract me from my country / Immortal my soul would yet yearn for it." Even palace life cannot distract the poets from love of the nation.

5. "By God, no other day but the Day of Independence / Shall Egypt celebrate with pomp and pageant."

6. "Red freedom has a door on which bloodstained hands pound."

How true you son of Egypt, son of all Arabs! The words of the great Tunisian poet are equally appropriate here: "If the People should one day choose to live, Fate must comply / Night give way to day and the chains that bind them break."

Chapter Eleven

I: That Which No Man Can Prevent

Two startled doves settled on the girl Nabawiya's breast. They delighted her. All alone, she stared at her breast and questioned them. "Why are you frightened? Why always on the point of taking flight?"

Nabawiya said to herself, "These two doves are stuffed with sand and hot pebbles." She grew bold and took a dove in each hand.

Hazina saw the birds on the daughter of her daughter's breast. She heard Shaykh Fadil's son calling out to the girl in a voice now grown rough as a reaper's scythe slashing through clover. "I must be vigilant," she said, and by way of banishing any evil thoughts she added, "Time and long intimacy have made the girl and boy like brother and sister."

Shaykh Fadil and the people of his house observe their son's constant proximity to al-Haddad's daughter and remark, "True, they were raised together, but he should pay attention to his studies. Science is a lasting occupation. The land will only crumble away with the coming days. The land will be divided between our sons and the sons of our sons."

None of the villagers see anything in the relationship between Shaykh Fadil's son and Nabawiya to merit the gossip of front porches or the conjugal bed. "A brother and sister. They grew up together."

As for al-Haddada, night and day she fans the flames of spite against Fahima's daughter in her son al-Sa'di's breast. "The girl is her mother's daughter!"

"I don't believe it," al-Sa'di said to himself. "Nabawiya of the oiled and braided black hair can't be like her mother Fahima. The nose, proud as a dovecote, the eyes, black as an impenetrable winter night; the long lashes are winnowing forks. It's the jutting top lip that worries me.... But it's impossible that Nabawiya be like Fahima! Nabawiya is a purebred mare that no one but I shall mount. She is my uncle's daughter and I am her cavalier. She is my steed and mine alone."

II

Suddenly, the boy and girl's encounters grow shy and confused. The body's temperature mounts and an obscure feeling of dread fills them. They need to move closer to one another, to feel the other's caress.

The boy said, "Oh how I wish we could undo what has been done."

And the girl said, "Our lost childhood, I wish we could bring it back."

III

A

The wind swept down like an unruly steed from its distant prison. It lifted the brittle twigs from the rooftops and wrenched the dead leaves from the branches of trees and brushed away the layers of fine dust on the ground. It flung twigs, leaves, and dust onto faces, houses, and rickety doors. It gathered up the few tufts of scattered gray clouds in the sky so high and the sky grew dark and heavy.

When the sky had wept its pure tears onto this earth clamoring with the iniquity of men, the indignant dust settled and cleared the air. The light spread, the wind went back to its fortress, the sky turned bright blue, and the children went out to look for scarabs and stones and rings and anything else that the secretive land of their grandfathers might have revealed.

B

Shaykh Musa, the beating heart of the village and its protector, departed this world two days ago. The sky wept on the eve of his passing by command of the Lord of Heaven and Earth, and to each his appointed time.

Muhammad the reciter had come as usual to sing the praises of the Prophet and the men had come as usual to perform the ritual dhikr invoking God's name. The time came for the shaykh to emerge from his seclusion—but the shaykh did not emerge. The night passed slowly and heavily but the shaykh had not yet revealed his radiant face to the ardent lover and the yearning disciple. All was still in the shaykh's room as the dawn lifted the darkness off the rooftops and palm trees and unveiled the faces of men.

Doubt assailed the hearts of those gathered and the lovers began to whisper amongst themselves. Voices rose and clashed.

"Let's break down the door."

"Who dares? Woe to him who tears away the veil!"

"Just yesterday I heard him calling on God, his beloved. 'Take me!' he called on Him three times in a voice loud enough for all to hear, a voice afflicted with passion."

"Lately, he talked a lot about farewells, about death, sunderer of loved ones and of brethren."

"Listen, maybe he's only tarrying in blessed Mecca?"

"No, this is his place and we are his heavy burden. We will wait for his return."

C

"O breaking day—how long you are, and you, coming night, how heavy. We cannot bear you, day that follows on night. O Lord God, You who conclude!"

"I smelled the body's perfume, but not its corruption."

"The bier flew off on its own!"

"We didn't carry the bier. It swam through the air like a speeding cloud."

"O black pit, and you—cascading dust, from you we emerge and to you we return. Here is the body. The soul has returned to its Maker. We recognize the true worth of men. Every year, on the anniversary of his death we'll celebrate with drums and tambourines and flutes. We'll race horses and do battle with canes. We'll perform the dhikr and feed the orphan, the poor man, and the prisoner in memory of his love."

D

The shaykh's loved ones—meaning the whole village—collected money to build the tomb. They consulted amongst themselves on the matter of the deputy who would accept offerings on the shaykh's behalf. Some said that the shaykh had taken to whispering his secrets to Khalil the whitewasher before his death. Others said that Yusuf Salim the butcher had always kept the faith and that the shaykh had honored him above everyone else by choosing a room in his house as a refuge in which to worship the One and Only. The discussion was resolved in the following way:

1. Only God can divine the dire consequences of the smallest departure from the true path.

2. The lover and the disciple who seek intercession should have the right to choose their preferred shrine.

3. Khalil the whitewasher will take up his place at the tomb and accept offerings there.

4. Yusuf Salim will take up his place in the room that was the shaykh's refuge in life and accept offerings there.

5. Yusuf Salim must never use the room for any worldly purpose whatsoever, and must undertake to respect its sanctity as long as it contains the belongings of the departed shaykh.

Chapter Twelve

I: The Meeting That Follows a Long Absence

The mother threw her thin-fleshed body into the arms of the son. She rubbed her head made heavy by the burdens of time against his chest and sniffed his clothes. She took note of the white hair at his temples. "This is what time has done to you and to me, my son. But you still bear the strength of two men in your arms."

The ghost of Bikhit al-Bishari, the father and the husband, whispered in the air. Fahima's ghost, daughter and sister, whispered in the air. The mother said, "My darling, my one and only." Their sobs rose and fell. "This is the station of joy, and this is the station of sorrow."

II

The loved ones all converged on the house of Bikhit al-Bishari. Mustafa and Hazina welcomed them and accepted their congratulations on the safe return and their condolences for the departed father and daughter.

Mustafa undertook his duties toward the deceased. He brought a reciter to chant plenty of verses from the Qur'an and he paid him generously. He visited his father and sister's tomb and recited the opening chapter of the Book and sprinkled water on their graves.

III

The Wafdist government kept its promise and gave a job to everyone who had worked in the British camps. Mustafa was hired as a janitor in the district capitol school, but he never went to town to take up his new employment. Could this be due to the paucity of dust, or perhaps to his proud contempt for lowly labor? Perhaps the hidden riches would soon emerge? In any case, Mustafa neither denied nor confirmed people's talk. The whole secret is hidden inside the deep well that is Hazina. The old woman's lips are sealed. She exhibits neither poverty nor wealth. She opens her toothless mouth as though to spit out her remaining teeth into the face of her interlocutor. "We live off my chickens and pigeons. I sell the eggs and buy what I need—may God deprive that other one (she means al-Haddada, sister of al-Haddad)—and my granddaughter Nabawiya weaves the best caps around out of fine wool thread."

IV

Gossip about the hidden riches increased and Hazina decided to pose the question to her son. "I have to choose the right moment. When he's in a good mood."

V

Mustafa was in a good mood. He began his reply with a loud guffaw. "Mother, are you anxious about having to support your needy son? Don't worry, a man's got his means. There's plenty of money in my head."

"In your head?" Hazina replied, astonished. "Plenty of money in your head?"

Mustafa laughed. "There's also lots of it lying around the streets, like pebbles."

Hazina pretended to be startled. "I beg the Lord to preserve your mind from insanity!"

Mustafa became suddenly serious and he put a hand on his mother's shoulder. "I'll never work for anyone again. I suffered so much in exile, mother. Bondage is bitter and from now on I'm a free man. You have no idea how ugly one man's dominion over another can be. Don't be afraid. I'll seek my bread from the streets like the birds and the prophets."

Chapter Thirteen

The river floods—covering the expansive sands there, on the west bank, with its copper-colored waters—and recedes, leaving behind fertile mud deposits. The farmer buries his watermelon seeds, whereupon the vines emerge and spread their green stems and leaves, then the blossoms burst open and the fruit reveals itself. The melons grow bigger and rounder; their outer skins are green but their insides are fiercely red, fiercely sweet, firm, and not too watery.

Boats bring the merchants who bargain with the landowners (not the farmers of course) and buy the crop. Then the same boats take the crop from the west bank to the east bank. They dock at the harbor; the porters empty their cargo and carry the sacks on their bent backs. They empty the sacks and separate the contents into piles: "Those are small melons and these are big ones. These are sweet and those are less sweet. And those over there are melons that split open during the journey."

The little merchants bargain with the big merchants: propositions and counter-propositions make the rounds, shouting and bickering and cries of, "God go easy on you! Thanks, but no thanks!" The bargain has been struck. The donkey drivers shout at their donkeys and the animals begin to pull the carts loaded with fruit. Wooden wheels creak over paved road and there, in Luxor, the sweet fruit finds an appreciative buyer who won't be stingy when it comes to paying for tasty and licit pleasures.

They are all there at the harbor: the big merchants and the small, porters and oarsmen, boat owners and cart owners.

And Mustafa—he's here too, in a shack he has made out of tall corn stalks. Mustafa sells tea and coffee to his clients. He also serves fried eggplant and boiled fava beans and chickpeas. This is the harbor and here is Mustafa. Mustafa's shack is covered with canvas that protects him from the burning sun in summer and the biting cold in winter. And here is a wooden bench and some mats for people to sit on—not to mention a set of playing cards for those who want some innocent fun, while those who want to gamble can go right ahead.

Your road to Luxor and the Tuesday market begins here. There is no other road to take but this one, you village- and hamlet-dwellers—whether you're mounted or on foot.

Chapter Fourteen
In Which All Threads Intertwine

I

A

Al-Sa'di said, "Mother, I want to marry my uncle's daughter."

Al-Haddada looked as though she'd been stung by a scorpion. "If you marry Fahima's daughter, you're no son of mine. I'll slaughter a pigeon in your footsteps, just as though you'd died or as though I had only given birth to girl-children, and God be my recompense."

The obstinate lover shouted, "Nabawiya is my cousin! She's my honor and my blood. Her flesh is my flesh."

"Nabawiya is Fahima's daughter, not al-Haddad's," the mother replied. "If you decide to be stubborn about it, I'll disown you."

The boy spit out his final words. "I don't care if she's the devil's own daughter! I'm the one who wants her, not you."

The mother turned her face away from her son in anger and the boy too turned and strode out of the house, slamming the wooden door behind him.

B

Mustafa—Bikhit al-Bishari's son from Hazina, and Fahima's brother—said to al-Sa'di, "Wait until my mother and I die.

Then you can ask Nabawiya for her hand and marry her if she's willing to have you."

C

Love and pigheadedness made al-Sa'di decide not to go back home. He said, "I'll build my hut far away from people, there, by the abandoned waterwheel. I'll grow my beard and my hair and pass the time with drink and drugs. Then the beast will burst free. He'll break down doors and leap over walls to get the thing he needs to stop his groaning belly. My chance is coming, it's coming, be it sooner or later. I'll snatch away she whom I worship and take her to live with me till the end of our days where the wild animals are. Between you and me, people of this village, lie the river and the sands and the vast mountains."

Al-Sa'di slept in the shade of the many-branched mulberry tree by the abandoned waterwheel, and he dreamt:

The mare bolted and threw Shaykh Fadil's son from the saddle. It shook the saddle off too, and galloped away, its mane standing on end and reflecting the sun's blinding light as though it were spun out of fire. People were running after the mare and Nabawiya, her hair loose, was among them. The mare reached the abandoned waterwheel and like a cat, al-Sa'di leapt onto her smooth back. He gripped her mane and whistled to her until she calmed down. Al-Sa'di held out his hand to Nabawiya and she took it in her own trembling hand. He lifted her up and put his arms around her. He tugged on the mare's mane, kicked her flanks with his heels and cried, "Hey, ho!" The mare sped off like the wind. She took him over the waters and across the treacherous sands to the very edge of the towering western mountains.

II

Mustafa forbade his niece to work in the house of Shaykh Fadil. He shouted in his deaf mother's ear, "Nabawiya is a big girl now, Mother. I'll repay my debt to Shaykh Fadil. I'll manage it somehow, God willing. I'm making a good living thank God, so why should Nabawiya have to work in other people's houses?" And he said to himself as he prepared to leave the house, "Al-Sa'di's made me realize that the girl has grown up and become a woman."

He issued orders to Nabawiya in a prudent, paternal tone. "No more going down to the river. I'll hire a water carrier. Go soak the beans and the chickpeas. I'll send someone to come and pick them up."

Nabawiya sat down and mourned her fate.

"I will remain here in this house until a suitor acceptable to my uncle and grandmother comes to take me to his mother's house. As for him, he will never ask for my hand. He is the sky and I, the earth; and sky cannot embrace earth until the Day of Judgment. I'll remain in this, my place, with my grief, soaking beans and chickpeas, sweeping and washing the dust from the house and listening to the old woman's talk. The old woman chatters on day after day and there's no one else but me to hear, day after day, that the past is sweet and the present bitter. Even the river has been denied to me, I, wool spinner, cap maker, and bird feeder, for they've hired a water carrier. Will he ever come to see me and bring me his clothes to wash?"

III

The large summer sun departed and the anchors followed in its wake. Big and small merchants, oarsmen, porters, cart owners, and drivers went off to God-knows-where. This is the winter sun with its laughing face and unfurled golden locks. And here are the tourists arriving from their dreary gray countries, lands of rain and white ice. They'll want to visit ancient ruins and ride in horse-drawn carriages. They'll want to buy and wear colorful caps, and travel in boats from the east bank to the west bank, and they'll fill up the hotels.

The summer sun took unemployment away with it and the winter sun brought work.

"Off to the hotel, boy! And you, old man, off to work! No more lazing around, people of Nejd al-Baharwa, summer is over. You're neither farmers nor landowners, so put on your white robes and turbans and wind your green sashes round your waists. Some of you will be bartenders, some will be waiters, and others, kitchen boys."

Mustafa mused aloud as he gazed at the river and as the men and boys passed by and greeted him. They all wore their white robes and turbans and their green sashes. "Because they have no work all summer and because they do have work in winter and make good money including tips, because summer must surely follow upon winter, they will want to gamble." Mustafa shuffled the colored cards and shouted at the river. "They'll gamble . . . gamble till the end of time!" replied the river.

"Those who work at night will come to my hut by day and those who work by day will come to me at night."

IV

All is dark around Hazina. The light has been snuffed out of her one good eye. Her one good ear no longer picks up the sounds of people's words, even when they shout. Nabawiya hides her swollen belly from her grandmother's feeble gaze in loose-fitting clothes. She gives vent to her pains in muffled groans—Grandmother might just hear her screams.

But when the girl repeatedly refuses food and vomits the little she does manage to eat, when she grows lazy and sleeps all the time, experienced Hazina is sure to notice that something is not quite right.

Amina the midwife came and shut herself up with Nabawiya in the bedroom. Amina came out alone and consoled Hazina thus: "God be with you. The vessel is cracked."

Hazina ground her remaining teeth and said to herself, "If I still had the strength I'd take care of the matter myself." She seized her cane and limped out onto the road to take the calamitous news to her son.

The End

I

Enraged Mustafa meted out the searing blows to Nabawiya and turned the lovely face into a swollen pulp. He gathered up the raven hair in two strong hands bulging with purple veins and threw the body desired by men onto the ground. He dragged her along, kicking the sinful belly over and over with his feet, then he left her there for a moment—a heap of broken-boned flesh moaning at the foot of the wall—in order to dig the pit.

He tossed the hoe aside, lifted Nabawiya and stood her up in the pit. Then he shoveled the earth back in over the body up to the neck, leaving the head exposed and the hair grazing in the dirt. Mustafa howled into the unknown, and Hazina translated her son's music thus:

"Not a crumb of bread, nor a sip of water until she tells who did it—until death."

II

Nabawiya fights off killing thirst—her throat is so dry, a whole year's worth of dryness—but she won't call out to beg for water. And Nabawiya is hungry (she craves the broken-horned candy bull in her wooden box). Nabawiya gazes at the little skylight high up in the wall—the one that lets light and cold into the room—and she says, "I no longer feel the cold."

"That light, is it sunlight or starlight? I don't care about the light itself. I only want to know if he's asleep or awake."

"How many days have passed since I've been here? Two days, a month, or a year? Many years perhaps? Those malicious eyes peeping in through the skylight, they demand his name and won't go away until I say his name. Not a word I'll breathe, since I'm done for, come what may. I'll never name my love or my furious uncle will kill him."

"Come closer little rabbit and bury your warm body in my hair. . . ."

III

Al-Sa'di kicked in the door of Bikhit al-Bishari's house with a ferocious blow. He stalked right by the seated Hazina without even throwing a burning, spitting glance in her direction. He knows his way perfectly well.

He drew, from between the folds of his torn robes, the sharp-toothed scythe and seized the grimy bundle of lunatic black hair as he would grab hold of a bundle of clover, and he sheared off the long proud neck. The dovecote tottered, the doves took flight, and the wolf howled at the sight of the spurting blood soaking his garments and running, snake-like, in the dirt. Howling, he carried off the head, its eyes still shining with life.

IV

A

Mustafa was washing plates, tea glasses, and coffee cups in a bucket of water. Around him sat the men, chatting, smoking pipes, drinking unsweetened black tea and coffee, and quarreling over the cards. But Mustafa is oblivious to this world—willfully so—and far away.

The devil with his filthy, matted beard and bristling hair suddenly appeared out of nowhere. Al-Sa'di spat in Mustafa's face, then he threw the beauty's head into the bucket with the glasses and cups and dirty water.

The men surround Mustafa with a deadly silence. They've stopped playing and talking but their eyes and faces speak worlds. Why don't they go away and leave him alone in this place till the end of his days?

Mustafa shouted at the silence and at the men and at all the village's inhabitants—women, children, houses, trees, and beasts:

"You all know who I am—all of you! I was a boy when I left for Sudan. I stood up alone and raised my hand against foreman Abd al-Dahir. I forced him to stand down. In my youth I've known as many women as the hairs on my head. In Sudan I slept in a tribal chief's bed—me, the little nobody, I slept in his bed I tell you! Chief of his tribe, commanding and forbidding, sentencing men to death and pardoning them as simply as if he were drinking a mouthful of water, but powerless to guard his own wife's cunt.

"Some of you know me from Palestine. You know that I married and that I couldn't secure my wife's cunt either. So I divorced her. Which one of you doesn't know women? I—and I know—married just once, and I'll never do it again no matter how long I live. I haven't even considered it in all this time, and I won't ever. Al-Sa'di is a boy and Nabawiya, a girl. Al-Haddad is his uncle and Nabawiya is not my daughter. She's al-Sa'di's shame first, then mine after him.

"I beat her and buried her alive in a pit without food or water so that she'd tell who did it. If I knew his name I'd tear him to pieces even if he were Pharaoh's own son. I'd drink his blood and no one would stop me. But al-Sa'di killed her before she could talk."

Mustafa felt as though he were wailing into the void, walking through twilight, creeping darkness behind him and before him with no end in sight. He felt that they had cast him out from amongst the ranks of men. This is their chance—these newfangled men of today—to break his swollen head. They have passed their sentence.

Mustafa snorted like a butchered cow: "I ... I ... after all these years ...."

He begged his self to give him his heart's desire—utter paralysis of speech and movement and sight—and his self complied.

The men carried Mustafa onto the cart. The mule pulled the cart and the wheels creaked at first then rolled steadily over the paved street, swerving suddenly at Shaykh Musa's shrine. At first the mule resisted the dusty descent but the driver's shouts and the hard blows he meted out with his green rod persuaded it to trot along briskly with its light load.

B

The time for tears is past and the light was snuffed out of your eyes long ago, Hazina. Here you are, after all these years, squatting in your house with the invalid son by your side. Husband and daughter have departed and the daughter's daughter has perished. Only the condolers and the gloating al-Haddada surround you now. No light, no fire on the hearth—what need for either fire or hearth?

The night with its stars passed away and the day with its sun arrived. The large frightened rabbit poked his head through the open door of Bikhit al-Bishari's house. Then he shot outside followed by the rest of the rabbits, big and small, and headed off in the direction of the copious grass in Shaykh Fadil's unfenced palm orchard—the one behind his house.

Short Stories

From the Dark Blue, a Story

All thanks to God, who has seen fit to strip me of every blessing but the gift of imagination.

—And prayers to the Prophet, who sheltered the gazelle when she sought refuge from the evil ways of her cunning master.

—And praise upon praise to you, my Prince.

(I say)

The perverse Italian count entered the City of Winter in summertime. Immediately the city's summer sun had stared long and hard at the stranger with its enormous eye and assaulted him with a thousand winks of light and a thousand winks of fire, he stripped off his clothes all the way down to his shorts (a modicum of modesty keeping these in place), stuck his bald head under a blue hat, and waved the hand that held a hubble-bubble. At this sign, a Scottish soldier in a blue-feathered helmet and a splendid blue suit, his sword hanging at his side, rushed over and handed him two bottles of whiskey.

The spirits-loving count drank one bottle standing up and one bottle sitting down on the airport steps. Then he rubbed his hands together and a blue carriage with blue curtains hanging in its fastened windows rolled toward him. An enormous man descended, picked up the count and deposited him in the back seat, while the Scottish soldier, sword drawn, preceded the carriage on his horse.

(I say)

The drunken count stood on the hotel balcony overlooking the Nile, and the Nile appeared to him in the guise of men clothed in the dark blueness of the waves circled by blue stars. At this sight, his heart overflowed, and he longed to act, so he drew the seven houses on paper, enclosed them in a flesh-piercing spiked iron fence, and set vicious flesh-tearing dogs at its gate. Each house of the seven had a garden and a pond with a fountain and ornamental fish, and there were also stables in the compound. The first house had one story, the second house, two (and so on: 1=1, 2=2, 7=7); and he painted the houses in descending shades of blue (from 1 to 7 or from 7 to 1). The count took off his monocle and chose six men: the mason, dexterous; the blacksmith, strong; the coachman, young; the farmer, virile; the house painter, cheerful; and the cabinet maker possessing a pair of marvelously talented hands.

(I say)

The count lay on his stomach on a rubber mattress full of cool air under a parasol from which hung strips of blue papier-mâché. Finally, he spoke, in Italian, "Bravo! You have put your faith in me and I have bestowed these houses upon you. Here you stand before me—gentlemen in black suits and polished shoes, blowing your noses in handkerchiefs. Everything inside this compound is now yours. Today we drink and make merry, and tomorrow I'll teach you how to play cards, for in a month's time we'll be hosting some very important guests. Each one of you will become an expert at holding a knife and a fork and at slicing the flesh from the bone. I'll sow the unconquerable spirit of solidarity in your scattered souls—the spirit that will make you the rich masters of a world that respects nothing but wealth and power; a spirit that I myself only managed to acquire after great effort and a life of squalor, nakedness, and hunger that nearly finished me off."

The count raised his glass, and the villains raised theirs. They toasted as though they had all been lords for ever so long.

(I say)

A month went by, followed by another and another, and behold, the gang received their guests—the world's richest, ever greedy for unthinkable profit—with hats in hand. They jabbered amongst themselves in Italian and spoke to the others in a mixture of Italian and Arabic. They played cards with the dexterity of magicians, excelling at the ballet of winks and nods that orchestrates the business of plunder. They drank the finest spirits (of wells and rivers and seas) to keep their heads from spinning and ate the choicest roast, fried, and boiled viands (of hills and mountains and plains) to keep their stomachs from aching.

(I say)

After praising you, my Prince, and praying over the Prophet, I offer thanks to God for this happy ending:

Here is the carriage approaching from afar with its blue curtains drawn, having first run over people and trees and beasts and fowl, and crushed countless anthills with its wheels. It stopped before the gate and the Leaders of Men— ever game—descended. The count raised his blue hat with one hand and waved the hand holding the hubble-bubble at the dogs, whereupon they immediately fell silent. "How quickly the appointed time has come upon us!" the count said sorrowfully to the men. No one replied, so he mounted the carriage and the men got in after him. The horses galloped off, kicking up a storm of dust that covered everything.

The Story of Abd al-Halim Effendi and What the Silly Woman Did to Him

I didn't see it, I wasn't there in those days myself, my Prince, but I was present at an evening put on by three of the very best storytellers who ever lived. Cruel death made off with them all in the same year (may God have mercy on their souls). The loss of them is great indeed.

—The one-handed man who played the lute, plucking tears from one string, laughter from the next.

—The mute who painted the world in shrieks and wild gestures—a world of seas and forests, birds and people.

—The toothless one who was an unsurpassed tambourine player.

After they had eaten a regal meal and drunk and snorted to their hearts' content, the mute let out a great shriek, whereupon the one-handed lute player strummed his lute and the toothless one slapped his tambourine to that fast-paced beat they call qadus.

And they began:

One night, on a night just like this one (and may the Lord of Creation bear witness to the truth of our tale) the English hopped off their rowboats and pitched their tents over there on the open stretch of sandy ground. There they remained for almost a month, the river running between them and the houses on the east bank, until it came to pass that a boy from the east bank spit on the ground and made a bet with his mates. He said, "What would you say if I crossed the river from east to west and came back again before my spit dries?"

The kids replied, "We'd call you a hero, and we'd tell the story of your exploit far and wide."

The boy said, "No. Say instead, 'Abd al-Halim Effendi did this and Abd al-Halim Effendi did that.' Give me the title of effendi, and call me the effendi."

The kids laughed. "So be it, Mr. Effendi. Just so, Effendi sir."

The boy pulled off his rags and threw his body into the water. He wrestled the waves till he arrived at the west bank with swollen stomach. He said to himself, "Here, on this fine sand, I'll stop to empty my bladder."

He heard the Englishman calling out to him in broken accents. "Don't be afraid. I'm the head cook of the English kitchens." The Englishman called out to him a second time in sinuous honey speech. "Praise to Him who fashioned your figure and drew your face!" Then the scarlet-tongued Englishman sighed, "Do let me touch your body and kiss your cheek."

To make a long story short, brothers, those sweet, colorful words spread the road leading all the way up to the English camp with a bed of musk and roses.

Now listen, listeners: The Englishman said to Abd al-Halim, "Go into the bathroom and take a bath," and he handed him a bar of scented soap. The boy went into the bathroom and scrubbed his skin red, expelling both louse and flea. He emerged in a pair of blue trousers, a white jacket, and slippers on his feet, and he sat down on a chair. Then the English barber came along and cut Abd al-Halim's hair and greased it with sweet-smelling pomade.

Those kids had laughed at Abd al-Halim when he said to them, "Call me Effendi," but now it's Fate's turn to laugh, for here is Abd al-Halim, a real effendi for all to see, waving his hands about while the English aide-de-camp brandishes his white handkerchief from a boat with its very own motor. Abd al-Halim Effendi went to see the town crier and the blind town crier made the rounds of the town's alleys. From his boat, the English aide-de-camp talked to the people with halting tongue. He asked them to build a stone enclosure and he gave them the silver coins, and he bought eggs and chickens from the mother and rabbits and pigeons from the daughter.

Pray over Taha the Prophet

In two days' time, the men had erected the enclosure and built the fine house in which the chief Englishman was to live. They also built the kitchen and the workshop and the warehouse and they repaired and paved the roads so that airplanes with propellers and airplanes with wings could land there.

In two months' time—thanks to the head cook of the English kitchens—Abd al-Halim learned how to prepare English food, how to make sweet pastry and savory pastry, and how to jabber in the language of the English, like the English themselves.

The teacher said to his student, "When summer comes, wear the light-colored sharkskin suit and carry a fly-whisk. There are a lot of flies about in the summer, Abd al-Halim." Then the foreigner said to the native, "And in winter, wear a dark suit—English wool, as you know Abd al-Halim, is the best wool."

Under the electric light bulb, body clung to body and the lover said, "If you befriend the important people, the little people will respect you. They'll stand to attention before you and they'll solicit your help. Help them, light of my eyes. Take their complaints to the important people who can solve problems and get people out of prison. If you take my advice, your name will ring out and your reputation, soar. That's when you'll have fulfilled all my dreams for you, Halim."

The days turned like waterwheels and the Englishman—Abd al-Halim's teacher—departed with the rest of his people to the land of the English. Egyptian officers now moved into the airport and ruled over it. The tears of sorrow that flowed heavily from Abd al-Halim's eyes on the day he bid farewell to his teacher, the Englishman, were rapidly succeeded by tears of joy as he heard the decree pronounced by the Egyptian officer-in-chief of the airport: "From today on, you will be head cook of the airport kitchens."

And so it came to pass, brothers, that Abd al-Halim took charge of the kitchens of Egypt's airport. He sits on a chair while everyone else works away, busy as bees. They wash dishes and dry them with towels; they scour the pots and pans, the knives and forks with Vim Powder; they peel the fruit, scrub the vegetables, and grind the beans; then they cook the meal so that Egypt's officers may eat.

Abd al-Halim's mother wakes up from a sweet sleep to the sound of the cock's crow and dawn prayers. She carries the red water pitcher in one hand and the white basin in the other, and she says in a low voice, "Abd al-Halim . . . ." Abd al-Halim wakes up, looks at his watch, and washes his face without getting out of bed. After drinking a cup of coffee with milk and sugar, he smokes an English cigarette with a black cat in a hat sitting on a chair stamped on one end. Then Abd al-Halim gets out of bed and shaves in front of a Belgian mirror. He puts on a clean, ironed suit. He drinks a cup of coffee with sugar, looks at his watch, and steps out to feast his eyes on the morning procession of girls coming back from the river with their clay jars. He gets into a boat that takes him from the east bank to the west bank and there, in the kitchen, he sits on a chair and looks at his watch. He asks them, "Have you boiled the eggs?"

"We've boiled them," they reply.

Then he asks, "And the butter and cheeses and jams?"

"In the dishes," they reply.

"Have you sliced the loaves?"

"We've sliced them," they reply.

Abd al-Halim Effendi looks at his watch again and says, "Now serve breakfast to Egypt's officers and bring me my breakfast too."

And so it goes, good sirs: Abd al-Halim Effendi breakfasts on the same fare as Egypt's officers: sliced bread spread with butter, a boiled egg and a fried egg, a plate of jam, and a slice of Romano cheese. Then he drinks a cup of black coffee and smokes a cigarette and looks at his watch and orders them about. "After you've washed up the dishes and the rest of the things, get such-and-such vegetables and such-and-such meats and such-and-such fruit." And this, gentlemen, is how Abd al-Halim Effendi chooses the day's lunch menu for Egypt's officers.

He looks at his watch and gets up off his chair, with someone or other always at his heels. Over at the fine house, he stands at the door and greets the lady of the house, wife of the airport's officer-in-chief, who says, "I want such-and-such vegetables and such-and-such meat and such-and-such fruit," whereupon Abd al-Halim says to his helper, "Go back to the big kitchen and bring me a basket with such-and-such vegetables and such-and-such meat and such-and-such fruit." While the helper is off on his errand, Abd al-Halim goes into the small kitchen and washes the pots, dishes, forks, knives, and spoons and he dries them with a towel. The helper returns and Abd al-Halim Effendi orders him to wash the vegetables and peel the fruit and brush the bottom of the pots with ghee and egg whites. Then he cooks the meal that the wife of the airport's officer-in-chief will eat along with her son Hosam al-Din and her husband, Egypt's leading officer. He then returns to the big kitchen to eat of the dishes that he has prepared for others.

The wife of the airport's officer-in-chief, my good sirs, was well-bred; a real socialite with scores of elegant lady friends, all smiles and perfume. Thanks to her, Abd al-Halim—who speaks the language of the English, excels at their dishes, and bakes the best pastries—came to know all sorts of important men along with their wives and sons. Thanks to her, Abd al-Halim's reputation took wing and soared as far as the cities. This is how the district commissioner, the chief of police, and the public health inspector got to know him—not to mention the wives of the district commissioner, the chief of police, and the public health inspector. The sons of the district commissioner and the chief of police also got to know him. Gabriel, the public health inspector, didn't have any sons who could get to know Abd al-Halim Effendi.

Nothing strange in all that, brothers, no spite or envy intended—it's just the plain truth. We tell it just like it happened without adding or subtracting.

The old man would stand up and stay that way until Abd al-Halim sat down first. The bandit's mother kissed his hand because he had gotten her son out of the dark labyrinths of prison. The bandit even came in person to kiss Abd al-Halim's hand and he publicly declared his repentance right then and there. Even the pickpocket kissed Abd al-Halim's hand, and he said, "You're the one who rescued me from the whip." The Friday preacher said this about him: "Abd al-Halim Effendi (who speaks in two tongues) is the very image of the grateful, devoted Muslim. He never raises his voice when he addresses the mother who reared him, and he thanks his Lord for having led him to the Englishman who taught him the trade that opened the doors of the very best people to him. He walks amongst us with the secrets of the grandest houses in his breast, but if we were to ask him about a certain lady who lives in a certain mansion for example, he would do nothing but sing her praises."

Now hear, O Listener, Abd al-Halim Effendi lived a life of privilege and ease amongst those folk, and these were his habits: After Egypt's officers had dined, Abd al-Halim would take the boat back from west to east, go home, bathe, and change his clothes. He would stroll through the evening trees to the Anaba Café and sit with his friends. He would play a game of backgammon with one of them and smoke a pipe. Then he'd play a second game of backgammon with another one of them and drink two glasses of French cognac while making witty remarks to the gathered effendis: "The only difference between an Englishman and a Frenchman is the Channel!" Then he would look at his watch, get up, and climb into a horse-drawn carriage that would take him back home again.

This is how the years passed and this is how Abd al-Halim's life proceeded apace. He never changed a single habit or detail—until the day a woman stopped him on his way to the Anaba Café.

The woman said, "My absent son, Abd al-Halim Effendi."

"May he return safe and sound," Abd al-Halim Effendi promptly replied.

The woman said, "This is a letter from him," and she handed a sheet of paper to Abd al-Halim Effendi. "I'm his mother, Abd al-Halim Effendi. Read it to me. Put my mind at rest and calm my burning heart."

Abd al-Halim Effendi was utterly confounded. He felt like a fish trapped in a net, and he said to himself, "This idiot, daughter of an idiot, is asking me to read, but I can't read!" He thought of his teacher, the Englishman, and silently reproached him: "Neither you nor I ever reckoned on this day."

The seconds flew by and the women started to get suspicious. "Why don't you say something, Abd al-Halim?" she wailed. "Speak, Abd al-Halim Effendi, and tell me—has something terrible happened to my son? Speak!"

Mild-tempered Abd al-Halim Effendi shouted at her. "Stop bawling at me, woman! I can't read!" And he threw the sheet of paper onto the ground.

At that, the anxious mother howled at the top of her lungs. "Oh! You've gone and died in faraway foreign lands, my son!"

Abd al-Halim Effendi clapped his hand over the woman's mouth. "Please don't shout," he begged. "You'll only draw a crowd of nosy good-for-nothings." He let her go, bent down, and handed her the paper. "I don't read or write, madam," he said to her. "It's just the clothes that make me an effendi, and now you see me ripping them to shreds right in front of your eyes."

Abd al-Halim Effendi never made it to the Anaba Café that evening. Instead, he went back home, shut his door fast, and curled himself up tight in his mother's arms.

That was the story of Abd al-Halim Effendi and the silly woman, my Prince. I've told it to you—I, who never witnessed those days—exactly as I myself heard it from the three storytellers, and may the Lord God be witness to the truth of the tale.

The Story of the Village Maiden

Safiyya

The orphaned virgin sells the baskets that her mother's mother twists out of palm branches in order to make a living from the toil of her arms and the sweat of her brow. Like all poor girls, she waits in a cage for a poor husband who will clasp her hand and take her to live with him in another cage. The days go by and the belle loses her pretty smile and her lithe figure. The days leave nothing in their wake but children, worn-out husband, summer and cold, pests, dust, rotted cheese, and a hand holding a crust of barley bread. For the impoverished girl, the only escape from the darkness of a destiny irrevocably etched into the tablet of the vast unknown is scandal. Then comes the dawning light, and her story is recounted in tales.

(When news of the poor maiden's beauty spread far and wide and finally reached the ears of the rich man in his palace, he loved her without having laid eyes on her, and he said to his messengers, "Bring her to me." When they brought her, the rich man saw the mane of a steed lying against the swan's neck and the red rose in the eye of a wild cow. "All praise to you, my Lord!" he exclaimed. "As though she herself were nature, the mother," and he sent for the judge. The judge came at once and wrote this in his book: "According to God's Law and the custom of His Prophet (best of men), the master of the palace and of its coffers has wedded the girl of the twin braids, sister of the sun and of the moon.")

Tuesday

The Leaders of Men meet at the stock market and play the game called "Man and His Fate" with strings and wooden puppets.

Whereupon,

—The butcher slaughters a cow.

—The price of tomatoes goes up from one piaster to two.

—The mother loses her son in the hustle and bustle of the Great Day so she asks the blind beggar for news.

—The orphans' sister shouts, "That swindler's scales are fixed, and he's sold me rotten potatoes to boot!"

—The runaway horse stretches out his neck and munches on a pile of grain. Blows from the canes of the dealer, the buyer, the broker, and the master of the scales rain down on him. He canters off, whinnying, "Never, but never, you lowest of men! Who among you dares to mount me and force me to pull a cart now that my master is dead?"

—The lunatic sings to the people leaving the marketplace from atop a wall in ruins:

Light the stove, Gouda
The worms have gobbled up the cotton!
The girls want to get married
But the boys aren't in the mood.

The sane man laughs at his idiocy, the educated man laughs at his poor prosody, and a boy throws a stone at him, while the woman who sells glass bracelets tucks a handful of dates into his lap and prays God to have mercy on her, her sick husband, and on the lunatic too.

Tuesday

Safiyya took the moneyed youth by surprise when she dealt him a painful slap on the cheek. His eyes spit fire and he shouted, "Beat her!" to his entourage, but they desisted for they saw that she was surrounded by scores of bodies ready to shield her from the fury of the male slanderer. He who had received the blow said, "By God, I gave her no cause." "Liar!" Safiyya replied, and the milk seller added, "He pinched her thigh." But the woman who had been standing right next to Safiyya said, "No, Umm Hafsa, he only flirted with her but she rebuffed him sorely."

The old man hammered the shoe into the ass' hoof and muttered, "All's fair in love and war, and a man's home is his castle."

After the Event

The sons of the poor crowded around Safiyya's closed door, seeking her favor, praising her virtue, and inviting her to come and live, proud as a queen, in the security of their embrace. "And who will feed the old grandmother?" she demanded. She evaded their proposals, addressing them in the manner of those who came before. "Every fruit has its season and every crop, its time of harvest."

Safiyya rejected the owner of two measly qirats of land, husband of two wives, and she nicknamed him "the Crow." To the wealthy old man she said, "Every grain has its own weight, Grandfather." When the moneyed youth—the one she had slapped in the marketplace for no reason—asked for her hand, she refused him, knowing full well that his only motive was that of revenge. He wants to lay a trap for her in the form of a document written by a shaykh and witnessed by witnesses. Then comes the disgrace to end all disgrace.

Felicity

Safiyya married a stranger from outside the village who had speculated in grain and cotton and thereby won the fortune, renown, and lofty position of a great merchant. He owned the house with high ceilings raised on white stone columns. Safiyya lived there, as the story goes.

(Her bed is soft—of ostrich feathers. She takes fresh fruit and stewed fruit for dessert. She eats meat from a copper tray, or grilled pigeons. Dresses of many colors, patterns, and fabrics fill her wardrobe and her ornament chest is shut tight on kohl jar, gold bracelets, and precious stones. A black slave sits at her feet and a white slave stands above her, cooling her with a fan. If she moans, a doctor hastens to attend and if she shouts the servants come running. If a sad thought dares to flit through her mind, she has but to look out the lattice-work window and gaze at the running water, the swaying trees, and the green dome of the sky.)

The Precipice

On the night of the full moon, it was Safiyya's habit to ride out in a carriage drawn by two white horses and a driver carrying a man-slaying gun in his pocket. From behind the lace curtains, she would contemplate the common folk, the palm trees, and the stray dogs scurrying, terrified, out of the path of the horses' hooves, the carriage wheels, and the whip. Safiyya would laugh out loud at the sight, but whenever she glimpsed the shadows squatting or sleeping in front of houses made of tin and cane, mud and straw, her heart trembled.

(Safiyya, these are your people, in spite of the life of comfort and ease that surrounds you. You have escaped their dark destiny, but chains of iron bind you to the bodies of your impoverished tribe; bodies riddled by the worms of the grave from time immemorial. The truth is the truth, Safiyya, so speak the truth.

The memory of the poor knows oblivion—unlike the memory of the rich, which knows it not: the rich folk never came to your wedding. Not a single rich lady came to visit you at the Two Feasts. When your husband lay sick, not a single rich man came to inquire about his health. Your husband is like you, Safiyya—the son of poor folk. The world opened its arms to him, as it did to you, one fine day.)

The Abyss

The revenge seekers expertly flung their nets around the husband and wife. Each withdrew into himself and hoped for better days to come. Instead, the days taught each to accept the other's vices and to resent his own. This is how they came to feel pity for one another, as well as shivering fear. This is how love—conjoiner of bodies and bestower of children—broke down and fell away.

The Farewell

As he made his rounds one day, the Angel of Death saw two desiccated, far-flung branches hanging from the Tree of Life, so he snapped them off and tossed them to the restless autumn wind.

An Embroidered Tale

His father used to pickle turnips and dye them with safflower petals before selling them. This, my Prince, was the first of a series of humiliating smacks dealt to Abbas by a ruthless, son-of-a-bitch world.

His father divorced his mother, Asma, after she had given him seven children who all died one after the other. Only Abbas remained to see his old mother, ragged and barefoot, collecting cow dung and hawking the fuel to one and all, even the stuck-up ones so long as they paid.

His father married a young girl — a tripe seller called Saliha — who was very hard on Abbas, given his penchant for playing war games and tossing firecrackers in their small, two-room apartment. Saliha the tripe seller gave his father a daughter whom he named Precious. Like her mother, she had a pretty face, a plump figure, and a dulcet tongue. Robes of flowing silk studded with sparkling sequins and soft as a poisonous snake's underbelly came tumbling out of her mouth every time she opened it. Precious was suckled on her mother's black milk. As for Abbas, my Prince, he was obliged to call her "Sister" and to call her mother, "Mother."

What a vile life! Such endless nights, such long days. And Abbas' skin is only human skin. Human skin is nothing like the skin of a doltish buffalo. Likewise, a human being in no way possesses the strength of a charging bull and therefore can't afford the luxury of a charging bull's wrath. You of all people know, Prince, that every black night is succeeded by a bright day and that all those black days have their white nights. That's how the little children of poor people grow up—smashing glass bottles in two and going out to meet the world on the streets in the guise of animals; men pecking away at their livings with the horny beaks of birds—bandits and ignorant fools. They avoid the naked light of day. Murderers that nothing but love's passion can finish off. Their purpose is chaos and the disruption of the peace of peaceful cities—that's why governments hate them and policemen chase them.

My Prince: it was inevitable that Abbas join that tribe of men when he did ("The streets are a thousand times better than home!") but with God's grace, Abbas chose the guise of the fox who only pretends to roll over and die. In this way, he won the favor of a pastry cook and became his apprentice. When the pastry cook's time ran out, he died. Abbas wept over him and so won the pity of a café owner who had been friends with the pastry cook. Abbas spent years at the café, first as a scullery boy, then as an assistant waiter and he got to know all the local good-for-nothings, the workshop and bakery boys, the drunks and the newspaper vendors, the fellow who badmouths his best friend behind his back, and the one who breaks chairs and knocks over tables if you get him angry.

Thanks to this very place, my dear Prince—a café with two doors, each opening out onto two different alleys—Abbas acquired three disguises: the guise of the cunning fox and the guise of the monkey and the guise of the cat with seven lives. He would take off one costume only to put on another, until the day when a car the size of a boat and the shape of a goose pulled up—over there on the street—and a well-dressed man got out. The man strolled from alley to alley as though he were gliding over water. When he reached the café, he suddenly felt tired so he sat down and ordered a glass of aniseed tea as a friendly gesture toward the culture of the common man. Abbas came over, welcomed him, disappeared again shouting, then came back beating out a rhythm on the tray with his spoon that would have happily sent a retired belly dancer straight back to the profession. The cheerful man—who was rich—said to Abbas, "Why don't you forget about the café and come with me?" Abbas whooped incredulously, "Me?"

That's what happened, my Prince, strange as it may seem. But it's a whore of a world, turning her back on you for years then suddenly taking you in her arms all smiles and jingling bells.

There, in the rich man's house, Abbas quickly learned the twenty-eight letters of the alphabet from which he fashioned ropes of colored beads to adorn the neck and wrists of the lord and patron who taught him how to hold a knife in his right hand and a fork in his left. The rich man always took his breakfast, lunch, and dinner at the Club with Abbas at his side: fried meats and grilled meats, duck and turkey and fish and chicken, and also fruit and wine. Between lunch and dinner they passed the time together—Abbas and the rich man—at the swimming pool among groups of scantily clad men, women, children, and lovely young girls. In two months' time, my Prince, Abbas had been so utterly transformed that none of his old acquaintances would have recognized him: a sensitive temperament, fingers soft as silk, a limpid soul that fell head over heels with any wet-haired maiden, and an endless passion for pictures and paintings, music and song, and the cinema in the East Gardens that showed talking films in Technicolor.

Allow me at this point to describe a film that Abbas went to see nine times and that pleased him to no end: Naked people wearing nothing but feathers, living in a forest, and killing off the outsiders with poisoned arrows. Suddenly, fully clothed people carrying rifles arrive on horseback and start shooting at the naked people, killing them all except their leader—the one with the most plentiful feathers. This one manages to dodge the bullets and jumps (suddenly) onto a horse faster than a motorcycle and faster than an ostrich. Then the villain—suddenly—abducts the gentle maiden who cured the men's wounds from the poison of the poisoned arrows and stamped a kiss on each man's cheek (except for the handsome youth to whom she gave the elixir of life to drink from her very own mouth because his wound was mortal). Now the handsome youth gives chase to the copiously feathered man on horseback in order to repay his debt to the gentle maiden. But no sooner does the handsome youth catch up with the villain than his horse tumbles (suddenly) into an evil, black-eyed ditch. Now the villain drives the maiden on before him as though she were a goat—Abbas can't make up his mind whether he's going to slit her throat or milk her. "Over here!" he yells at the handsome youth and points to a hidden cave. The villain suddenly tears off the maiden's long gown and his eyes grow wide with lust: a tree bursting into tongues of red flame and cleft asunder into a pair of smoldering legs. "Hurry up!" Abbas screams at the handsome youth. "Don't give up!" he shouts at the maiden, at which she picks up an axe. The villain keeps coming closer, nailing one and all to the ground with his terrifying demon-eyes. "It's none of our business!" they all cry, but the blameless bare-thighed maiden—symbol of resistance—still clutches the axe in her hand. Suddenly, the brave, handsome youth strides in and kills the villain in order to spare the beautiful heroine from having to become a murderess. The film ends, my Prince, with a long kiss—the kind of kiss that makes people like to see films and that induces our modern makers of films to end their films with kisses that make us like films.

After having seen this particular film—and this is what made me tell you the story of the film in the first place—clever Abbas grew even more skillful at fashioning speech. He twisted out of words ropes with which to hang a man, tie up a mule, bind a wild animal, and cordon off a street. He also came to excel at composing thrilling stories about heroes doing battle with savage beasts and making shoes out of their skins.

That's exactly how it was, my Prince! But I've forgotten to tell you about the rich man. . . .

He lived in a house with four floors and four balconies to each floor. The house had a garden with barren trees and trees that bore perfumed blossoms. The rich man loved his own kind, but chastely. He wore a suit of armor; he touched no one and let no one touch him. He simply loved and languished like the narcissus flower that desires only itself and the river. This is how he lived with Abbas, until, quite out of the blue, the day for whose sole sake stories are told, epics sung and men go mad overtook them both.

She lived on the fourth floor of the house opposite and Abbas saw her and said, "O light of my eyes!" whereupon she slammed the balcony door shut and disappeared. On the second day (it was a Tuesday) she rose again like the morning sun and Abbas said, "O light of my eyes!" whereupon she departed angrily without shutting the balcony door. Wednesday was evidently a day of protest, but she reappeared on Thursday and only looked as though she were angry. As soon as Abbas opened his mouth to speak, she turned her back and the whole operation was repeated in this way for the next two days.

On the Christian Sabbath, she looked out with a face all blossoms, passed her hand over her lips, and blew two flowers into the air. Their perfume made Abbas dizzy but he quickly recovered and begged her for an urgent interview at the Club. She refused with a toss of her head and flung back a strand of her hair. Abbas eagerly pressed his suit: "At the East Gardens Cinema." She refused with another toss of her head and flung the same strand of hair forward into her eyes. Abbas opened his mouth and closed it again when she pointed to the garden and drew the shapes of the trees and of the sunset with her hands.

Oh dear! Would that that meeting under trees set on fire by the setting sun as it strikes the houses of the masters had never taken place!

O my Prince! The husband was a master; a liberal man of middle age who had taken every precaution to protect the honor of his pretty fifth wife from the recklessness that possesses every pretty young girl, from the innate weakness of the female sex, and from the tricks and stratagems of impudent scoundrels like Abbas. He had fenced off the house and fortified the fence with steel and barbed wire and trees and alarm bells and black dogs and black cooks and black servants.

This gentleman of middle age owned an ivory cane which he used to brush away flies and to beat men, my Prince—a cane that made all who saw him fear him and respect him and above all, make way for him, whether he was out walking for exercise or riding in a carriage driven by a whip-wielding coachman. And so it was inevitable that Abbas should fall prey to this very cane. He moaned and groaned from the painful blows and he called out to God in heaven and to any and all merciful earth-bound mortals for succor, till the good Lord sent him a policeman who dragged him off to the station—not as a lover, mind you, but as a would-be thief. From the station, he went directly to the hospital (in the company of yet another policeman), it having been established that he was indeed a thief, and not a lover.

Once his wounds had healed, he discovered that he had become an animal in an iron cage. A stranger stood by the cage and cursed him roundly to an assembly of stone-faced men dressed in priestly black robes. The men listened gravely from atop a raised dais. They nodded their heads and murmured amongst themselves and their leader pounded his gavel when the stranger (who never ceased cursing Abbas) grew overly enthusiastic in cursing Abbas's mother and the pastry cook and the café owner. The cursing man demurred and said that they—Abbas's mother and the pastry cook and the café owner—had planted the seeds of evil in Abbas's soul so that when the generous gentleman extended a generous hand to him, Abbas—who was like a son to him—bit it and bloodied it and utterly destroyed the good rich man's life, for the gentleman now suffered from a trauma that might well oblige him to submit to a severe medical regimen for the rest of his days—hot milk mixed with whiskey and cardamom seeds—and to quit forever all the good things of this radiant world, "as your good honors certainly know."

The most amazing thing of all my Lord Prince, was that the cursing man narrated the smallest details of Abbas's life to those in attendance, which surely demonstrates his vast authority and his wide knowledge of the many secret books and files in which Abbas's biography and the biographies of many other sons of Adam besides Abbas are recorded!

And now that I've told you all, my Prince, I'll finish up the rest of Abbas's story: his tender years and his single offence shielded him from a prison sentence. As the judge said, "In spite of the life he has lived, he has not understood a mustard seed's worth of the way of the world. We therefore sentence him to a reformatory for young people that will educate him, improve his morals, and remake the human being in him."

Abbas held back the groan that came to his lips. He listened to the iniquitous sentence passed upon him by strangers at the instigation of a cursing man no doubt in the pay of the husband of his adorable beloved, the one he shall never forget (for love doesn't just die off at a moment's notice).

How true it is that man is not the master of his own destiny, for here you are Abbas, an adult they treat like a child whose life from now on at the reformatory will be in the hands of people much like most people—cruel and without pity. And even if they do have mercy on you at the reformatory there will be no wine, or meat or paintings or music or balconies or hot baths or cinemas like the one in the East Gardens that shows talking films in Technicolor.

Well, my Prince! Neither you nor I expected this unhappy ending.

A Melodramatic Story

The House

In Fustat it was. Two floors of white stone, on each floor four rooms with high ceilings. The upper floor for living, and on the lower floor, a storeroom, a granary, a toilet, and a reception room. The reception room was the farthest room in the house. It was close to the toilet and the bathroom and intended for the accommodation of male guests.

The house belonged to a noble family of old. Long ago, a Turkish lady possessed its keys by right of marriage. After her death, it passed to bungling heirs who sold the house because of a dispute over repairs to the wooden staircase that joined the two floors.

Its enormous door is made of tamarisk wood, secured from the outside by a chain of sturdy links fastened by a big lock. From the inside, the door is secured by a bolt. The visitor must knock on the door with a wicket set in an iron-handled knocker, and wait. The people of the house examine him first through a peephole in the middle of the door, so as to distinguish between friend and foe.

The Ironer of Fezzes

The new owner of the house is a devout Copt. He chose to live in Old Cairo so as to be close by the Babylon Fort, the monastery, the cross, and the crucifixion. He turned the reception room into a shop and he lived on the ground floor with his old mother. When she died, he could not bear to live alone in the big house, so he repaired the staircase, married a young Coptic girl, and lived with her quite happily on the upper floor. She is the mother of his son, Girgis.

Girgis and the Game of Time

He inherited the house from his father as well as the profession, but the hands of arrogant time lifted the fezzes off the heads of peaceable folk, blessed the bootlickers, and pounded in the heads of the fez-wearers (vain men, stubbornly clinging to an age that's dead and buried). And here is Girgis, ironing a lady's scanty negligee, a girl's short skirt, and the shirt of the bareheaded man of the house (how this arrogant, double-dealing cog of a world creaks and turns like a mournful waterwheel!).

Murqus is an Upstanding Citizen

Murqus—son of Girgis and father of Hanna—gathered all the living members of his family and lectured them on the necessity of selling the shop as well as all the other rooms on the ground floor. He said, "You are the sons and daughters of the Ironer of Fezzes. Insolent time has obliged you to bow to its will. Say with me: 'All praise to You in Your sovereign kingdom, Lord God who tries us, for this is Your wish.' You created Hanna—our son and the bearer of the family name— a trusting fool who can't tell the difference between a dog and its tail. If it weren't for the loving and ever-watchful eyes of his family, he would surely wander off and lose himself in the hustle and bustle of the streets.

"Here I stand before you today, an old man with bent back and no strength left in his bones for work. But let not despair take possession of your pious souls: know that Hanna, our son, is at least fit for marriage. It is our duty—the sons and grandsons of the Ironer of Fezzes—to help him and await God's reward. And now, come, children of our Lord God, and eat of the good things I have prepared for you: pork and mutton, summer fruit, wine, rum, and brandy (and candles for the statue of the Virgin)."

Muhammad Kumbul the First

The new owner of the ground floor is stout, with a stomach and heart of plastic, one glass eye and one squinty eye. He hides his eyes behind a large pair of black sunglasses. He owns a house in Bab al-Sha'riya in which lives Zibda, the mother of his children, with her family and his family. He also owns an apartment in Frenchman Suleyman Pasha Street in which lives with his mistress, the discreet belly dancer who aided him with unparalleled devotion in his 'business' dealings in Beirut before the start of the civil war there. He has hard currency in faraway banks and floating currency scattered in various stock markets. With his money he transformed the ironer's shop into the Miami Boutique: he trapped the light in glass cages and in their colorful waves swim feminine underwear, perfume, cosmetics, electric hairdryers, and packs of Kent—the ladies' preferred brand of opulent American cigarettes.

The Business Agent

On the morning of the grand opening of the Miami Boutique, the workers came and sprinkled sand out front. They festooned the place with garlands of flowers and hung

Muhammad Kumbul the First's portrait with the following encomium printed in large letters underneath: "Head of the Family and War Hero of July, May, and October—and all the other months of the year too."

On the evening of the day of the grand opening of the Miami Boutique, Muhammad Kumbul the Second descended from his shiny black American car. He came forward, surrounded by a gang of sturdy friends and underlings, and cut the ribbon while the cassette player blared out Muhammad Kumbul the First's favorite song: "The tub told me, get up and have a wash, girl . . . !"

On the morning of the day after the grand opening of the Miami Boutique, all three dailies printed a photo of Muhammad Kumbul the Second laughing, surrounded by a laughing crowd of people. They also printed an advertisement for the Miami Boutique, and here is its text: "Muhammad Kumbul and Brothers brings good news to the residents of Old Cairo. Mr. Kumbul has moved his Beirut business, and now, with the dawning of a modern era of openness and competition in Egypt, he is taking his first steps on the new road of Science and Faith."

Three Fingers

Muhammad Kumbul the Second (whose nickname was Three Fingers) gathered up his colored prayer beads and tucked them into his pocket. He took out his handkerchief—releasing a cloud of French cologne into the air—blew his nose, rubbed his hands together, and assumed the manner of Muhammad Kumbul the First. "Empty the containers into the warehouses," he said to the men standing next to the two trucks, and he pointed to the ground floor of the house.

The Last Supper and the Last Sunday

From the moment that Hanna saw money, his interest in those colored bits of paper with pictures stamped on them grew and grew. His mind now wandered whenever he sat down to eat and drink with his family and consequently, he was unable to share in their boisterous extravagance. Hanna demanded of Hanna, "How can I get at the purse stashed above the wardrobe without them noticing?" After a great deal of thinking, Hanna replied to Hanna, "When they've gone to bed." Hanna felt anxious, so he got up and sat down and got up and sat down again. "I wish they'd go to bed," he said. The sound of his family laughing or coughing or chewing or sipping had become unbearably oppressive to him. So he begged the Virgin, Mother of Christ, to help him. Meanwhile, his family ate and drank and ate and drank with the appetite of the deprived who want nothing more than to go on sating their hunger and slaking their thirst for ever and ever. Finally, the government ambulance came and took them away—insensible and clutching their swollen bellies—to the public hospital, where they all died.

Hanna, the Last of the Living

He stepped over the empty bottles, the paper bags of mangoes, the scattered pear seeds, and climbed onto a chair—that's how he found himself on top of the wardrobe. He untied the purse, took out the money, and stuffed it into his pants pockets. He was careful to dodge the Virgin's watchful eye.

After Hanna had crossed the bridge, he headed for the movie theater. He had often hung around under its large billboard—the one with a picture of scantily clad girls, laughing and frolicking in the sea's angry waves.

As Hanna came and stood gaping, so did the police in their police car. The moment the eyes of the undercover detective fell on Hanna and noted his shoddy clothes and his anxious manner, he took him for a young vagrant.

At the station, they searched Hanna's pockets, took the money, and stashed it in the government safe, which they double-locked. As for Hanna, they chucked him, teary-eyed, into the same dark, damp, narrow, lice-, ant-, bedbug-, flea-, and bat-infested cell with scoundrels, thieves, homosexuals, alcoholics, machos, cocaine addicts, and heroin addicts. Two days later they led him, teary-eyed—and this is the end of the story—to a government reformatory that will teach him a trade and good conduct in the society of men.

The Song of Elia the Lover
(To the pure-hearted and empty-headed ...)

It was a hot evening, just after sunset, and contrary to habit Elia the lover was wandering about aimlessly. Elia the lover was sad because Samia—the girl he loved—wasn't walking by his side at that very moment.

Elia the lover wandered aimlessly down the street lined with the most movie theaters in the city. His right hand was snuggled in his right pants pocket and his left hand was snuggled in his left pants pocket. The transistor radio nestled in his black and white striped shirt pocket played a tune dedicated to the Ismailia Football Team, which had just won the African Champions League. Elia was thinking about Samia and feeling like the most miserable of God's creatures. Luckily so, for if he hadn't felt miserable, he would have been even more miserable. He would have accused himself of having betrayed his darling Samia—who wasn't walking by his side at that very moment.

All those people wandering around the same street as Elia were crowding up the street. Some people were coming out of a movie that had ended at six and some people were about to walk into a theater for the six o'clock show. There were those people standing in front of the brightly lit plate glass shop windows, contemplating men and women and children's shoes and also handbags and perfume bottles and watches and rings and radios and television sets and refrigerators of all different sizes and brands, and underwear and outerwear for both sexes and all ages and tastes. Some people were just standing outside and looking, some people were walking in and buying, and the shops all had names like Mickey, Rivoli, Star, Happy Home, and Silver Shoes.

All that Elia the lover could do, now that he was alone and now that Samia—his favorite sweetheart—was presently with her family in the South (and therefore not walking by his side) was look about and read the shop names as well as the posters and ads glued onto walls and lampposts and ask himself, the Holy Father, and the Holy Mother, "What shall I do?"

He stopped in front of a poster of a guerrilla carrying a rifle, and one of a trench-coated French actor (the mysterious type) starring in a film in its fourth consecutive week at Cinema Ramses. Also playing for the fourth week at Cinema Miami was the girl that people called the "Cinderella of the Arab Screen" wearing a backless swimsuit and lying under a beach umbrella with the foaming sea spread out in front of her. A very clean kid was sucking Astra milk out of a baby bottle and smiling. Then there was a wind-battered tent and a girl whose clothes were torn and she was surrounded on all sides by the desert and by barbed wire.

Elia tried to cry. He wanted to but he couldn't. A piece of orange rind stuck in his teeth was bothering him. He looked for it with his tongue till he finally found it and spit it out, feeling the kind of relief you feel when you manage to get rid of a minor irritant. Then he remembered Samia , his darling, and he got upset again. An idea came to him and he put it to work immediately. He conjured up the image of the director of the Ataba Post Office — Samia's father's boss and the one who ordered Samia's father transferred to a small post office in a small town in the South. Elia spat a second time.

The man was fat, clean-shaven, with a big round belly under his black jacket. He had a round head, a thick neck, a frozen, waxy face, and he owned a car. Elia kept raising his hand and jabbing the air with his index finger as he explained the situation. At first he was a bit bewildered but then once he had convinced himself of the justice of his case, his tongue relaxed and the words poured out of his mouth quite easily. The waxy face kept its silence, which greatly annoyed Elia, so he cursed and spat for the third time.

That was the first time that Elia the lover — under the lights and in the crowd — really felt alone. Above the shop signs the colorful neon billboards flashed on and off so as to astonish country folk and small-towners. If Samia were with Elia, they would search out those astonished faces and glance at each other and smile. That was just one of the many little games that filled their lovers' hearts with happiness. But Samia is with her family in the faraway South, where a man sleeps with his rifle and his wife, children, sheep, cow, dog, and donkey all in one room; where wolves and foxes slink down paths too narrow for people to walk, and where it's next to impossible for you, stranger, to distinguish between man and beast or people and objects. Elia is under the lights now, and Elia is alone, and Elia is sad.

There, on the left-hand sidewalk to Elia's right, the streetlights were lit up. The streetlights on the right-hand sidewalk, down which Elia was strolling, were not lit up. This was standard wartime procedure in the big city—followed by the small towns then the villages near and far—in a war against a dastardly enemy who wouldn't hesitate to kill civilians and who really does kill them. The street lived on nonetheless, as was its wont and as it had done for thousands of years. The radio crouching in Elia's black and white striped shirt pocket was also alive, moving fast. The man who was singing stopped singing and another one started talking:

"Arab press and broadcast media have pointed out that hostile Western news agencies who support the enemy and their attacks against our military, economic, and civilian installations now recognize that the apparent normality of the Egyptian street represents the most effective resistance to the Israeli bombardment; an offensive which, according to them, will not lead to an easy victory since it has failed to produce the necessary psychological effects. The Israeli plan to destroy the Egyptian regime has failed."

In spite of the enemy, all these people to Elia's right and to Elia's left and in front of Elia and behind him form lines and cue in front of the soft drinks vendors' stalls. There they put out the fires raging in their breasts with bottles of Coca-Cola, Pepsi-Cola, Lemon Siko, Orange Siko, Strawberry Siko, and all sorts of other types of cold drinks, except beer, which is only served in well-lit cafés with spotless glass windows. The owners of these cafés have to procure special licenses from the government permitting them to serve alcohol to their clients. The legal punishment for serving any alcoholic beverage to an underage customer is a fine for the first offence then closure of the premises for the second.

This situation used to create problems for Elia the lover in the past. His baby face and his less than average height don't square with his real age (which finally put him in the ranks of men only a month and a half ago). That's right, Elia would wiggle out of fix after fix by producing his identity card at just the right moment to reveal his age and profession—a respectable civil servant with a salary at the beginning of every month. And if Elia hadn't been the oldest child in his family and the only son and breadwinner, he'd be a soldier now and living the rough life of soldiers.

Samia knows this from the letters that will one day stop coming. Samia cries a lot. "Love is stronger than death, love is stronger than death!" she repeats over and over again. Then comes the inevitable oblivion.

This is how Elia's thoughts made him sad all over again.

It surprised Elia the lover that these subjects—such as whether he was a man or a boy—should preoccupy him just now. He was quite aware of his own insecurities (which his identity card mostly took care of) but how was he supposed to act in front of his mother? Was he a boy or was he a man? Just yesterday he had watched the film censor in a rare television appearance, with all the excitement of someone with a personal interest at stake. The censor was a young man dressed in a black suit and a crooked tie. He said, "The reason we rate some films 'for adults only' is that we want to protect young people from horror films, gangster films, and pornography." His colleague, who was a psychologist, addressed himself to the hostess of the show, the one with the lovely white teeth and the pretty smile. He added, "Youngsters are innocent. Their minds can't handle the same pressure as adults." The hostess presented the third guest to the censor, who smiled and said that he already knew the third guest quite well. Then the hostess smiled and her white teeth shone as she presented the third guest to the viewers. She said that he had studied sociology at one of the most prestigious American universities and that he had only just returned the day before from a six-year fellowship abroad. "Five years," the sociologist interrupted, by way of correction. The hostess smiled and then everyone laughed loudly. The sociologist chatted with the other guests for a while, then the camera zoomed in on him as he turned to the audience. "Children are like monkeys—they love to imitate, so it's quite easy for them to turn to criminal activities. We must do our utmost to protect them and to protect society at large. This is exactly what the law is trying to achieve and what our legislators are trying to achieve when they make the laws, and that's why we need to punish those who break the law in due measure." Everyone agreed and the program ended.

It was the day before yesterday and not yesterday as Elia had imagined. He had stopped by his aunt's house after saying goodbye to Samia, who is down South now with her father the post office employee who was transferred because of his hot temper and because he couldn't get along with his boss, the director of the Ataba Post Office. This is what makes Elia the lover feel lonely and sad under the lights and in the crowd. This is what makes Elia wander the streets aimlessly.

Most of the young men milling about in front of the second-class movie theaters were underage. All they had to do to get into one of the 'adults only' movies was pay the theater usher half a piaster and walk right in. Elia the lover smiled and said to himself, "If that girl Samia was with me now, we'd go see an 'adults only' movie together and we'd celebrate our generation's victory over the censor. We'd walk into a café with glass windows and I'd drink beer and Samia would eat ice cream or drink lemonade or maybe even beer if she wants.

"I'd spend the pound note that's in my pocket as well as that ten piaster note and then I'd be broke and happy," he added. "But Samia's not here with me now—she's off over there in the South with a hot-tempered father and men who veil their faces and carry rifles. Samia has to face the beast all by herself." Elia sighed. "My poor darling Samia!" And Elia the lover fell right back into his lonely gloom.

The young men wore either short-sleeved shirts or long-sleeved shirts or shirts with the sleeves rolled up. Since it was altogether usual that they should feel hot during this particular month of the year, they had all absolved themselves of having to button up the topmost button of their shirts. Set free in this way, their bare chests emerged, sometimes crowned with hair, sometimes fuzz, but most often just smooth and blank. The neon lights bounced off those chests and made their skin shine. Elia saw a chest black as marble and one that was dark brown like the foam on a cup of coffee and one that was just plain brown and a golden brown one and a pale, yellowish chest, and one that was just pale. Chains sporting a little silver or bronze or copper or real gold or fake gold Qur'an or crucifix hung on some of the chests. Romantic songs playing on record players or tape decks or radios drifted out of some of the shops and into Elia the lover's ears, reminding him of his dear Samia. From time to time, the radio squatting in Elia's pocket interrupted its normal broadcast with a military bulletin. Elia the lover felt that this was somehow quite appropriate to the general melodrama of life and to the nobility of his own sad situation. For this reason, Elia the lover listened to the bulletin with an expression that made all who saw him more than ready to bear witness to the fact that Elia the lover was exceedingly interested in politics.

"But has the beast truly gobbled up Samia?" Elia the lover asked himself, and his heart beat fast. He decided that he didn't believe in such nonsense, that he was just trying to frighten himself in order to indulge in some gratifying self-torment. Elia prefers Samia to all the other girls because she is the only girl in the whole world who loves Elia in spite of his thick, black, frizzy African hair. Samia loves Elia more than any of the creatures scuttling about on this planet. And Elia wants nothing from this world but Samia. From this moment on, Elia will live on the memory of Samia and he'll stay true to her forever—just as they'd agreed.

They each pricked a finger. Elia drew a heart pierced with an arrow and wrote his name and Samia's name on a piece of paper with his blood and he gave the paper to Samia. Likewise, Samia: she pricked her finger and drew a heart pierced by an arrow with her blood and wrote Elia's name and her name and presented the paper to Elia.

Elia will keep that paper till the end of time because of the happiness of the happy moments that Samia has given him, lying on the grass in the park, sitting side by side in a dark movie theater, or strolling along the Nile. Elia moved as lightly and as elegantly as a sprite. He felt quite happy standing, sitting, walking, or watching a football game. Samia is pretty: average height, dark-skinned with rosy dimpled cheeks. She is neither short nor fat and her soft, shiny black hair looks perfect braided into two long braids. Nevertheless, sometimes her face contracts and purple shadows appear under her melancholy black eyes. When Samia pulls her hair back in a bun, Elia looks at the bun and thinks it doesn't suit her, but when she lets her hair hang loose down her back and over her shoulders and then braids it all up, Elia imagines the head of a proud and noble mare and Samia's face goes back to how it was before.

Elia wishes that he could believe in the furious beating of his heart, a herald of their meetings, when Samia would suddenly appear before him just as he liked her to be: with low-heeled shoes (like a boy's) and no socks and a skirt above the knee or a miniskirt or a micromini or pants. He would take hold of her hand and they would fly off above people's heads just like angels do in paintings, and they would drink beer together with his pound note and the ten piaster note.

Samia is the third girl that Elia has ever fallen in love with. The first one was called Hoda and she was a friend of Elia the lover's sister Hoda and also her classmate in junior high school. The second one was called Amal and she was a friend of Elia the lover's sister Hoda and also her classmate in junior high school. And finally Samia, who was a friend of Elia the lover's sister Hoda and also her classmate in junior high school. Samia is still in school now because she likes school and because her father can afford it. As for Hoda, she's still working in a textile factory along with Hoda, Elia the lover's sister. Elia said to himself, "No doubt my sister Hoda is in love with a young man from the neighborhood or from the factory where she works and maybe even he's still a student. But Hoda is sharp and knows how to keep herself to herself."

Elia the lover silently reproached his sister for not trusting him even though she knows he knows the meaning of love. He decided he was wrong to tell her about his three love affairs, then he decided he wasn't wrong, then that he was, then finally that he wasn't. Hoda is afraid of her mother, who worked as a seamstress after the death of her husband—Hoda and Elia's father—until her eyes went bad. She did it all for Hoda and Elia's sake, and she turned down a lot of suitors so that he and his sister wouldn't end up suffering the fate of children with stepfathers—the street and all kinds of abuse. That's why sometimes his mother is hard on Hoda, because Hoda is a girl, but she loves Hoda and Elia. Elia disagrees with his mother sometimes and agrees with her other times, but he loves her always. And he loves Samia more than Hoda, his first sweetheart, and Amal, his second sweetheart. Elia clasped the bronze crucifix hanging on his chest—the one Samia had given him—and he said, "If someone offered to exchange this crucifix for one made of pure silver—or even of twenty-four carat gold—I would refuse. This crucifix is an important symbol of the great love between me and Samia." When Elia realized that he had just pronounced Samia's name—far away now—sorrow and loneliness descended upon him once more.

Elia the lover reached the end of the street lined with the most movie theaters in the city, and he said to himself, "It's only right that Samia's father was transferred from his job at the main post office in Ataba to a small branch in the farthest South because he's hot-tempered and can't get along with his boss, but that's no fault of Samia's! What's she got to do with it, poor Samia?" He walked down an unassuming side street (even though it did have a National Bank on its corner surrounded by floodlights powerful as the sun's rays). He walked and thought and the light gradually grew fainter. He said, "Ever since Samia left I haven't been able to so much as look at another girl besides Samia. Oh you devil, Samia, you. If only you knew how much I love you and how devoted I am!"

When he reached the middle of the street Elia turned and wandered down an equally insignificant street. He felt the fierceness of the shadows and he tried to remember the name of the street, but he couldn't. "Now I know for sure that I have a conscience," Elia declared. "I haven't looked at a single girl since Samia left. After I broke up with Hoda her blue eyes started to make me feel uncomfortable. As for that girl Amal, as soon as she got the chance and met that handsome European-looking movie extra, she broke up with me and said she was going to be a movie star one day and buy a red sports car and a villa overlooking the Nile, and drive the car and look out at the blue water every morning from a window with real flowers in the window box." Elia, devoted as a brother to Amal, shouted, "That boy is a liar!" But Amal firmly and emphatically replied that it had nothing to do with any boy and that she had been to Cinema Cosmos to see the girl who had grown up in the slums, become a famous actress, and now drives a red sports car and owns a villa overlooking the Nile with real flowers in the window boxes. Elia, devoted as a brother, bellowed at her, "That's just the movies!" And he said to himself, "Amal is done for."

He had reached the end of the dead-end street by now, so he turned off into the street that led to the bus stop. A group of sanitation workers were fixing the sewage pipes. They had hung up a glass lantern painted red. Faint red spots bounced off the lamp and struck Elia's eyes, which seemed natural to Elia since it was just a battered old lantern burning dirty petroleum. The lantern hung on a wooden scaffold that cut off the street right in the middle. The words CAUTION: DANGER were scrawled on the scaffold in red letters. Pedestrians were evidently not forbidden from crossing, however, because nobody stopped Elia, not even the policeman who was drinking tea from a tin mug. He didn't ask him for identification or where he was going or any of the usual demands at that time of night. The policeman was busy talking to the sanitation workers whose mixed accents told Elia that they came from the South and from the Delta and also from the very same city in which Elia lived. Samia used to live in it with him too and they were happy alongside its kaleidoscope of human inhabitants, southerners and sanitation workers and policemen and Muslims and Copts and rich people and poor people and Arabs as well as foreigners; a vast city full of taxis and private automobiles and wooden carts and tramways and trolleys and buses and bicycles. "Cairo is a symbol of the whole of Egypt," Elia the lover mused as he walked on, and he started thinking about mules and donkeys and horses without really knowing why except that he was confused and in love. So he went back to thinking about mules and donkeys and horses, most especially their proverbial stupidity. It astonished him that these stupid, miserable, illiterate animals didn't simply tumble into the many ditches and sewage works that the sanitation workers were constantly fixing. And Elia pictured a whole host of mules, donkeys, and horses sprawled out on the ground, because of the muddy, slippery streets (for example) or because the loads pulled by the stupid, miserable, illiterate animals were just too heavy.

Elia the lover started thinking about his darling Samia all over again and he imagined Samia laughing at the sight of him falling into a ditch being fixed by sanitation workers. He decided that the shame of it would maybe send him running, never to return and look upon Samia's face again, except after a long, long time. Maybe he'd just never see her again at all and look for another girl with his sister Hoda's help instead. Elia the lover decided not to think about it anymore. He wondered whether he was just one of those people who are terrified of both doubt and certainty. He smelled Samia's breath in the air around him and it occurred to him that he hated the smell of hunger and that every mouth has a scent usually masked by the act of chewing. He remembered that he liked the scent of Samia's mouth and that Samia had stopped eating eggs for his sake, while for her sake he always chewed gum before their encounters.

He said, "The day I have a decent salary I'll marry Samia, and her father will accept it as well as her mother, and my mother too because Hoda will be married by then and my mother can support herself from her sewing and in any case, all she cares about is my happiness and Hoda's happiness." Elia ran toward the approaching bus, which was already crowded because now is the time when everybody needs to spend some time at home—even the ones who are in love, like Elia.

Mr. Sayyid Ahmad Sayyid

I

The apartment has two rooms. It is a dilapidated place, located in one of the city's old popular quarters. It belongs to the two sisters who inherited it from a dead father and a dead mother. The older sister lives in one of the rooms and the other room is rented out to Mr. Sayyid Ahmad Sayyid.

Yesterday, the younger sister (an old woman nonetheless) came to visit her older sister and for some reason known only to the Great Knower, an argument broke out between them.

The younger sister said, "You live in one of the rooms, and that's your right. It's my right to rent the other room—the one that Mr. Sayyid Ahmad Sayyid lives in." The older sister—and she was lying—replied, "Mr. Sayyid Ahmad Sayyid hasn't paid last month's rent, nor this month's rent either." The younger sister shouted that she would evict Mr. Sayyid Ahmad Sayyid. The older sister pointed out that this wasn't entirely feasible just yet. "Wait another month." Then the younger sister could send a warning notice with the bailiff followed by the sequestration order followed by the legal letter of eviction.

II

Mr. Sayyid Ahmad Sayyid trembled as he listened to the sisters. It was winter and pouring endlessly outside. A vague fear had accompanied him from childhood on: something terrible would happen to him all of a sudden—something well-planned and executed—and no matter how hard he tried, he would never be able to stop it. Mr. Sayyid Ahmad Sayyid touched the large scar just above his left eyebrow.

It was a rainy night like this one, and too dark to see properly. Instinct guided him along the narrow, serpentine alleys whose potholes and passageways he had long ago memorized. His feet were weighed down by the malodorous mud that made his stomach churn and his heart contract dangerously. Suddenly, a live body slammed into his, and he heard a woman scream. When he opened his eyes again, there was light—yellow light, like the sparks from the clash of rusty swords. He saw lamplight pouring in from windows and doorways. He did not move a muscle. There were men and boys and women blocking off all the exits. He didn't resist. He was powerless to defend himself with his tongue, which seemed to have frozen in place. When he came to, his whole body was shaking like a kettle of boiling water on a stove. They had bound up his head with a tattered rag and rubbed coffee grounds into the open wound. He tried to move his lips, but the old patriarch of the house stopped him. "She told us everything, son. She said that you didn't intend any kind of whoring." Mr. Sayyid Ahmad Sayyid heard the women make sympathetic clucking noises. He wanted to sleep, but instead, he started to cry like a baby.

He would really like to go out now, but it's dark and wet and muddy. He would like to walk on and on in un-muddy, un-guarded, brightly lit streets. There he would find an empty bar—empty even of its bartender—and drink and drink because his body is thirsty for drink. Instead, he reluctantly went back to reading his book, *Bonaparte in Egypt*. The following anecdote—narrated by an Italian pharmacist—impressed him greatly:

> "Everybody is afraid. All they talk about is troubles, public misery, thefts, and murder. Nothing is safe—neither life nor property. They shed a man's blood as if he were an ox. The police officers, on their rounds day and night, judge, condemn, and execute their sentence in an instant and without appeal. They are accompanied by executioners; the instant the order is given, some poor devil's head falls."

The author went on next:

> "Are the striking similarities between those days and our own merely a matter of coincidence? Perhaps the above words are nothing more than the simple impressions of an Italian pharmacist; an all-too-eloquent individual, like the Frenchman Bonaparte himself, who declared the confiscated lands of the Mamlukes national property, while in reality they were disposed of to satisfy that moloch, the army's cash reserve, and the fallah continued to be a fallah."

Here, Mr. Sayyid Ahmad Sayyid left off reading. He had heard footsteps. He stared hard at the person—completely unknown to him—who entered the room, then he closed his eyes and shouted, "The last phrase, sir, represents the views of the author of *Bonaparte in Egypt*, and not mine in the least. As for Bonaparte, this is what he had to say about Egypt to the directors: 'This nation is completely different from the idea our travelers have given us of it. It is calm, proud and brave.'"

III

Mr. Sayyid Ahmad Sayyid was on the point of speaking out against the threats of the younger sister (who declared that she would smash his head in) but he held his tongue when the older sister winked at him. Here he is now, safe and sound, zigzagging through the alleys with *Bonaparte in Egypt* tucked under his arm and heading for the cafés downtown because he's got a friend over there. Mr. Sayyid Ahmad Sayyid's expectations of sudden catastrophe decrease significantly during the daytime.

IV

Here is a café and here is a friend.

The friend was in a bad mood. "Something wrong?" Mr. Sayyid Ahmad Sayyid inquired.

"A family matter," the friend replied.

Mr. Sayyid Ahmad Sayyid started tapping on the table with his fingers. The friend said, "That's annoying. Please stop."

Mr. Sayyid Ahmad Sayyid stuck his hand in his pants pocket and jingled his loose change. He fixed his eyes on the crab-like stain on the café ceiling. The friend got up and hastily said good-bye. Mr. Sayyid Ahmad Sayyid asked the gaping waiter for a cup of coffee, lightly sweetened. "I questioned him anxiously and he responded listlessly," he mused. "I've annoyed him. He left in a hurry as though he were afraid I'd run after him—as though he were healthy and I was a leper. He's upset me. And I don't even want a cup of coffee. I only wanted to get rid of the waiter."

V

The waiter seemed to have disappeared and the political friend kept his silence. Mr. Sayyid Ahmad Sayyid repeated his order to the waiter, and the waiter shouted, "One coffee, light sugar!" Mr. Sayyid Ahmad Sayyid tried to draw his friend into conversation. "Such a fuss about nothing . . . what's this? Nixon's victory over McGovern, and the Jewish vote . . . ? American presidents are all actors playing a role on the stage of world politics! They are quite simply the servants of American capital, my friend. When will we ever learn that America will never support us Arabs against Israel even if an angel with snow-white wings wins the presidency? That's just the nature of the regime, my friend. It's capitalism. It's America that comes between you and me, my friend."

The friend mumbled something and took out his pack of cigarettes, lit one for himself and put the pack back in his pocket. He sat lost in thought for a moment, then he took out the pack and offered a cigarette to Mr. Sayyid Ahmad Sayyid. The waiter came back with the coffee. Mr. Sayyid Ahmad Sayyid took a sip then addressed his friend in a whisper. "In a city like this one, it's the little things that kill a man. I asked for a cup of lightly sweetened coffee but here I am nonetheless drinking a cup of coffee with extra sugar."

The friend said, "Never mind."

"I should have never accepted his cigarette," thought Mr. Sayyid Ahmad Sayyid. "Maybe it pained him to have to offer me one. But really, he didn't seem to care one way or the other. I also failed miserably at getting him into a conversation, even though I said all sorts of things to please him. At any rate, I believe in what I said and that's enough for me." And he said to his friend, "I'm off. I've got an appointment," he lied in order in to cover up his embarrassment.

"Sometimes I sit here—you know," said the friend.

Mr. Sayyid Ahmad Sayyid said, "I'll pay for the coffee."

"Don't bother," said the friend.

VI

There is a café . . . and here is a friend.

The merry friend said, "I don't have any money."

"I don't want any money," replied Mr. Sayyid Ahmad Sayyid.

"Not even for bus fare?" the crafty friend asked.

"I have money, I really do," insisted Mr. Sayyid Ahmad Sayyid. He clapped for the waiter, ordered himself a cup of coffee and asked his friend if he wanted to drink anything. The friend laughed and said to the waiter, "Two coffees, light on the sugar. The gentleman is paying," and he pointed to Mr. Sayyid Ahmad Sayyid. A lame lottery-ticket seller came into the café and the friend bought a ticket. Then a beggar woman came in carrying a child whose face and limbs had been horribly disfigured. "I know her," said Mr. Sayyid Ahmad Sayyid. "She's a refugee. Those burns on the child's body are from enemy napalm."

The friend smiled spitefully and said, "She would make a good wife and mother and you would make a good father to the poor kid. The Israeli Air Force hit the Canal cities with all kinds of bombs, but not napalm. What happened to the waiter?" he added maliciously. "Hmph. Call him—go ahead, call him. I'm your guest after all."

Mr. Sayyid Ahmad Sayyid called over the waiter, repeated his order and took three cigarettes out of his pocket. He gave one to the waiter, and one to the friend, and lit the third one for himself.

"How's your love life?" the friend asked.

The waiter came back with two cups of coffee and two large glasses of water. Mr. Sayyid Ahmad Sayyid took a sip and said, "This is a cup of coffee with medium sugar. If that devil had only put in one half teaspoon instead of a whole teaspoon, I'd be drinking lightly sweetened coffee."

The friend repeated his question. "Your love life—how is it? I'm talking about her. The mystery woman." It was as though Mr. Sayyid Ahmad Sayyid was an actor in a stage melodrama— that's how the friend saw him anyway.

Mr. Sayyid Ahmad Sayyid shouted, "It's a sad thing to concentrate all one's feelings on a single person, in a single heart."

"Who said that?" the friend asked. "It can't be you at any rate."

Mr. S. pointed to the book, *Bonaparte in Egypt*, and replied, "Bonaparte said that in a letter to his brother Joseph."

The friend laughed and said, "Yusuf. Yusuf, Mr. Ahmad."

"Don't make fun of me, my friend. *Bonaparte in Egypt* has lots of passages that describe our own times perfectly. Really significant passages. If only you'd listen and think. Please! Don't take me for a fool." And with that, Mr. S. started leafing through the book and reading out loud.

"The author writes, 'Had their hearts been as anachronistic as were their institutions, they would have fought, regardless of the outcome, as had their predecessors. But their hearts were modern.' General Cafarelli wrote, 'I maintain that the laws which sanctify property sanctify usurpation and theft.' Bonaparte said, 'The sea, of which we are no longer master, separates us from our homeland, but no sea separates us from either Africa or Asia. Our enemy is strong but we are numerous; we have enough men to form our cadres, and we have no lack of munitions.' Kléber said this about Bonaparte: 'He is incapable of organizing or administering anything; and yet, since he wants to do everything, he organizes and administers. Hence, chaos and waste everywhere. Hence our want of everything, and poverty in the midst of plenty.'"

Suddenly, a large crowd of people spilled into the café. The friend jumped up as if he had been stung by a scorpion. "Today's football match will be on television in a little while," he said to Mr. S. "I'm going to watch it at home."

Mr. Ahmad laughed and said, "Take me with you. This is my chance to ride in an empty bus."

The friend replied in a sentimental tone, "If I let you, you'd read the whole book to me. You'll go blind with all this reading. Believe me! Why don't you write instead? Ha!"

"I haven't got any talent, my friend, no talent at all," Mr. Ahmad replied as he trotted after his speeding companion.

VII

They waited for a long time but the bus still hadn't arrived. The boy had long hair and sideburns. The girl was short-haired and she wore a short blue skirt and a white blouse with a red necktie. The boy said to the girl, "If we'd taken the tram . . . . Didn't I tell you? We should have taken the tram."

The girl answered the boy, "And walk two stops? I'm already late and Mother knows what time I get out of school."

The boy said to the girl, "We'll take the tram then walk two stops together."

"The bus will be here soon," the girl said coquettishly as she toyed with a necklace from which hung a small Qur'an.

The boy, who had misunderstood, said, "I don't give a damn!" and he stamped the ground with his foot and stalked off.

The girl hugged her schoolbag tightly to her chest in order to hide her breasts from the stares of the angry man who had been following her conversation with the boy. He was wearing a coat with a stiff collar and his forehead was stamped with a dark blue prayer-mark. When the man didn't budge, then spat on the ground, the girl ran off to catch up with her friend.

The bus came and everyone pushed and shoved each other. Mr. Ahmad didn't manage to get on. He looked right and left and realized that he had lost his friend, and that this was exactly what the friend had wanted all along. So he turned his face in the direction of a nearby café and as luck should have it, he found another friend.

VIII

The radio was broadcasting the football match. The friend was following the game on the radio but also reading about it in the evening paper. The rest of the paper lay on a nearby chair. Mr. S. asked his friend's permission to have a look at it. The friend replied, "Take it. Keep it."

Since the newspaper now belonged to Mr. Ahmad, he carefully cut out one of the advertisements. The friend watched him sideways, then snatched up the clipping thinking it was something worth looking at. When he discovered his mistake, he tried to hide his embarrassment by reading the clipping out loud. "Tomorrow evening, grand charity soirée organized by the Egyptian Women's League in the Arabian Nights Ballroom of the Nile Hilton Hotel. The event will raise money for the League's new headquarters. Dinner will be followed by a program featuring Egypt's most celebrated performers."

The friend let out a nervous laugh, and Mr. S. said, "Maybe she'll be there." Deep down he felt miserable because he was still powerless to speak her name. He explained apologetically to his friend, "Yes, I mean Madame Tampier, the athletic beauty—one of the stars at the Cairo Tivoli. It made her furious when Bonaparte declared that all women were naturally cowards. She could never bear an insult to her own sex, so she publicly challenged Bonaparte to a duel and vowed that her pistol would speak for her. Not all women are afraid of men—not even of Bonaparte himself."

IX

At the bus stop, Mr. S. recounted to a friend he met there the story of the boy and the girl and the angry religious man. He said that the girl's fingernails were long. The friend inquired about the significance of this observation, and he replied that the author of *Bonaparte in Egypt* (an Englishman) had said ("and don't just content yourself with the surface sense here, my friend"): "The long fingernails of Egyptians are not only ornamental. They are also weapons against the dust."

X

The old lady said to Mr. Sayyid Ahmad Sayyid that her sister— "May God not return her"—had gone back to her house in the neighboring district. She said that her sister suffered from a serious heart condition and that she was sure to die sometime during the coming year. "But she's all alone," and God was just to have denied her younger sister children who would have inherited her.

At St. Helena, Napoleon said to his companion Gourgaud, "In this world, one must appear friendly, make many promises and keep none."

J. Christopher Herold—author of *Bonaparte in Egypt*—said to Mr. Sayyid Ahmad Sayyid:

"Posterity would be impressed by the depth of their acumen and vision. Cambyses, Xerxes, Alexander the Great, Amr and Selim I all invaded Egypt from the Gaza Desert."

The stranger who suddenly entered the room asked Mr. Sayyid Ahmad Sayyid, "Tell me—who exactly is this Xerxes?" Mr. Sayyid Ahmad Sayyid buried his head under the covers and replied in a stifled groan, "I don't know! I don't know!"

Ruffin concluded his report thus:

"When I took my leave from him, I was given neither sherbet nor perfume, nor handkerchief. The absence of these marks of honour confirmed my impression."

The Ghoul

The outcast stood erect and spit on his merciless people, and he threw a parting glance at the distant houses. But how great was his joy to find that his pregnant cat had followed him, and he marveled at the devotion of animals.

He walked on, and she walked on after him. They walked for a long time until they penetrated the heart of the wasteland and vicious thirst and hunger seized them. The cat had given birth to a litter of tiny, blind kittens. She satisfied her hunger with the flesh of one of her brood and slaked her thirst with its blood. The outcast did the same as the animal. Raw flesh did not appeal to him however, so he struck two stones together and lit a fire with the brushwood he had collected and roasted a kitten and ate it. Then, when cruel thirst assailed him, he drank the blood of another victim.

This is how the days passed, until the day that the outcast and his cat fell at each other's throats. The outcast emerged victorious and he devoured the cat's flesh. Our friend, a son of the times, now faced hunger and thirst and solitude and fear of the wild beast all alone. He bit his nails and gnawed his fingers, then he lit a huge fire to frighten off the beast and to guide the traveler lost in the wasteland—for the outcast thought he might one day decide to return to the world of men.

When he finally stood face-to-face with the lost traveler, fear of this return gripped him, so he felled his brother and drank of his blood and devoured his flesh, raw and roasted.

With the passing of time, this became his habit and this, his nature. His fame spread far and wide once he took to hunting in the world of men. People grew skillful at describing and depicting him, and mothers invoked the Ghoul to frighten their disobedient children and to caution their traveling husbands, fathers of their sons.

Tears

One day, a man cut off a viper's tail with an iron bar, so the viper fled his house and took refuge in the house of an old widow.

The old widow, who was wise, said to herself, "My chickens are my livelihood. I barter with the shop owner. He takes the eggs and gives me a packet of tea and a cone of sugar and a box of matches. Likewise, the tinker: he takes the dung of my chickens and gives me a needle, a spool of thread, a handful of salt, and some grains of pepper. Vipers are companions of the grave. They are messengers of death to this world, spraying their poison from deadly fangs. Vipers like eggs cooked with onions. I'll cook an egg with onions every day for this viper."

This is what the old woman did, and the days passed in this way till one day, the viper laid her speckled eggs and hid them as any viper mother would do. Soon afterwards, little worms appeared, twisting under the feet of the peaceable chickens. It wasn't too long after that that the worms turned into vipers slithering about in the corners of the tranquil house. One morning, the old woman discovered a dead chicken, and she sat down on the dusty ground with the dead chicken in her lap and wept over her helplessness, her lack of judgment, and the ignominious fate of an old woman obliged by fortune to face the offspring of a tailless viper.

The viper whose tail had been cut off by a man with an iron bar took the scent of the dead chicken, then she gathered her brood and sniffed them one after the other. When she discovered the culprit, she seized its neck with her fangs and strangled it to death. The constant viper then departed with the rest of her offspring to the undefended open spaces, while the widow wept in her tiny den with her chickens and two corpses and no end to the tears in sight.

This is how the separation came to pass.

Fear

A barren shop owner married a beauty and he watched over her as he did his goods. The beauty is a framed painting to be admired but not to do any admiring; a precious object in an opulent home with warbling birds in cages and colored fish swimming in a glass bowl. Chains of magnificent stones adorn the beauty's throat; anklets of silver and bracelets of gold bedeck her. She wears costly brocade and brilliant scented kerchiefs embroidered with sequins and pearls.

The days—as wills the Maker of Days—are divided between morning and night. The mornings of our man the shop owner are bright—bright with the light of the heavens and bright with profit whenever the people are obliged to crowd round goods grown scarce. The evenings, however, are full of whispering goblins.

When night falls, the master of the house (possessor of wealth and guardian of beauty) floods the place with burning light and unleashes the snarling dog. He undresses his paramour and toys with her and gratifies her with sweets and fruit and licks and sucks. Once the husband has reached the summit of his pleasure, he sleeps and snores—until this night passes and a bright new morning dawns bringing bright new profits in its wake.

In this manner the days turned on themselves until one night, the snarls of the faithful dog roused the shop owner, terrified, from his bed. Here are shadows moving in the burning light (perhaps in search of wealth, or perhaps in search of beauty) and he is so very jealous of both wealth and beauty.

He threw everything within reach of his hand at the shadows till one of them fell and was carried away by his two companions out of the light and into the dark. The shop owner slept no more that night. When morning came and he saw the blood stains on the carpets, he cleverly surmised that this blood that had flowed from the shadow could well lead to the shadow's death. Now, his fear of the revenge that the two other shadows might exact on behalf of their dead friend grew and grew. So he bought a rifle capable of dispatching a couple of souls, and he stopped trading and shut up his shop. When night comes, he sits wide awake, clutching his rifle so as to protect wealth and beauty, and from time to time he fires two bullets into the air.

Death

It is related that, wishing to toy with the souls of a male and a female slave who worked in the fields of the master, the scowling angel Azrail disguised himself as an old and bearded blind man with a tablet under his arm and a quill and compass in his hand.

Astonishment possessed the two heedless slaves: What need does a blind man have for a tablet, quill, and compass? And why does he not feel his way with a stick, like other blind men?

The female slave said to her husband, the male slave, "If you command me, I shall question him." But the angel—who had overheard their conversation—said, "A slave never questions, my child."

"Are you a master?" the male slave asked.

"I am a master not to be questioned and a slave who does not question," the angel replied. The two slaves knelt down and said, "How wise you are! Teach us, O wise one, a useful maxim."

The angel said, "You will be responsible for your wife's death, and she for yours, O slave."

"Explain your enigmatic words, O wise one," begged the slaves.

The wise one replied, "I'm thirsty and a draught of water from the master's well would slake my thirst."

"We'll give the wise master to drink from the master's sweet well," the two slaves declared.

The wife lowered the bucket into the well. As she drew it up, she spotted a large fish with shining eyes swimming in the water, so she dropped the bucket and descended the steps that led down into the well. She was not clever enough to realize that the angel Azrail can turn himself into a large fish with shining eyes, artfully dodging and biting whoever tries to catch him.

When the fish bit her, she screamed, "Help me, Husband!" The slave husband hastened to rescue his slave wife, and he climbed into the well. This is how the angel Azrail dispatched them both: he drew in a deep breath that gathered up all the pure air, heaved a deep sigh of poisoned air, and suffocated the two slaves in the master's well.

Be a Good Egyptian: Be the Master

He married—having fled his people—a beautiful bride who had also fled her people, and he promised her a home.

So he put on the cloak of a regal beast of prey and headed for the wilderness, and there, where he found water cleaving the rocks in two, he built his house and enclosed it in thick coils of interlacing trees.

The lost traveler came and asked for food, and he fed him without demanding payment. The lost traveler departed, then returned with his family. He thanked him and his family thanked him. He fed them again, and they insisted on paying. This is how he set up the Eat and Give Thanks Tavern that became an oasis for travelers.

He and his wife took turns sharing the work, but when he weighed up the difference between the woman's profits and the man's profits, and compared the folly of the drunk to the shrewdness of the teetotaler, he decided that his wife would do most of the selling. He pressed her: "Reel in the client with the magic language of your eyes, but don't ever lie on your back or we'll lose everything and be forced to return to the way we lived in the bitter old days—me, the male rat and you, the female rat—with nothing but disgrace for company."

At the insistence of those clients who wanted a place to spend the night, he built a two-story hotel topped by a third elaborate story with a labyrinth of halls and chambers.

And so it was that he erected a whole world unto itself: food, drink, dancing, sex, and sleep and children (these are his grandchildren and he is their acknowledged grandfather, they play in the sunny vineyards and wait upon his stony smile).

A chicken lays eggs: the eggs hatch and chicks emerge— that's how money produces more money. If you don't use it to exploit others, they'll use it to exploit you. They are the majority and you, the minority. You are an individual and they, a collectivity. That's how it is with the collectivity—if you buy up a small bit of it, the rest shall submit to the will that builds and plants and uproots and negotiates. They will be the mouth that chants your praises.

He asked her, "Why do you need a name? Why do I need a name?"

She replied, "Call me 'Virgin of Paradise'—for I'm a nymph in the water—and I'll call you 'Majesty' and in this way we'll recognize each other always. Don't lose your way and don't beat the drum. Be guided by your sun."

Do you understand, or shall I repeat myself, Majesty?

The Messenger

The messenger of death (the swindler, the able one) removed his silken garments, his ornamental necklaces, earring, and anklets, and disguised himself as a live fish swimming in sweet water.

The messenger of death (the swindler, the able one) removed his silken garments, his necklace and earrings.

The messenger of death and lover of ornament (the swindler, the able one) removed his robes of silk, his necklace, earrings, and anklet and disguised himself as a large live fish swimming in a sweet-water well. "Come," the master of the house called out to him in the language of the fish. The messenger, reaper of souls (the swindler, the able one), removed his robes of silk.

Translator's Afterword

Yahya Taher Abdullah was reputed to have the remarkable ability of memorizing his stories and reciting them perfectly by heart at the lively literary gatherings that were a hallmark of the Cairo cultural scene in the 1960s and 1970s. Reports of these legendary performances point to one of the key elements of his style and of his persona. Abdullah was a poet, a master craftsman of language steeped in a centuries-old oral tradition, a modern-day heir to the itinerant balladeers who performed the ancient epic cycles of North Africa and southern Arabia in Egypt from the fifteenth century onward. But he was also a consummate storyteller who expertly mobilized the formal resources of the traditional Islamic tale to create a richly ironic and distinctly modern literary language.

This very special achievement is reflected in his biography. Abdullah was born and grew up in Egypt's deep south, in the ancient village of Karnak, a small and insulated community of peasant cultivators with ties to the thriving tourist trade of the neighboring town of Luxor. In 1959, at the age of twenty-one, he moved to the district capital of Qina, and five years later, in 1964, to Cairo, where he launched his literary career with the virtuoso public performances that brought him to the attention of established writers like Yusuf Idris and Abd al-Fattah al-Jamal. There he remained until his untimely death in a car accident in 1982. During those eighteen years, he produced five collections of short stories and four novellas while living a precarious social and political existence. Unlike many of his peers, he never held a steady job and his writing was his only source of income: he was a literary vagabond of sorts. On the other hand, he suffered the political fate of most of the young leftist writers of his generation who lived through the 1967 war with Israel and the disastrous results of the 'Open Door' social and economic policies of the following decade: persecution, imprisonment, and increasing marginalization.

From the deeply conservative rural south to the cosmopolitan hustle and bustle of the great capital city of Cairo; from the stark, millennial ruins of an ancient civilization to the flash and glitter of modern-day palaces of consumer capitalism; from the primordial agricultural rhythms of the Nile Valley to the abrupt historical catastrophes of war and occupation—these are the landscapes Abdullah traverses effortlessly in his writing, carefully illuminating the changeless human dramas and passions that lie at the core of them all: love and greed, fear and death, but most of all, the will to power—to dominate and exploit, to 'be the master.'

Abdullah's very modern worlds of social conflict and individual alienation are mediated through a much older narrative language; the ritualized, communal language of the public poet and storyteller. It is the language of the great epic cycles of rural Egypt, of the *Thousand and One Nights*, and of Sufi song and liturgy. Repetition, rhyme and rhythm, paronomasia, alliteration and invocation, the finely turned proverb, and the coded archetype are its building blocks. Abdullah takes this narrative repertoire and distills it into a supple and sharply honed modern idiom capable of expressing a whole range of moods, from comical pathos to scathing parody. He strips his prose of the expansive temporal and descriptive conjunctions and clauses that characterize the formal written language, inviting the reader to infuse these absences with his or her own emotive and poetic responses. His phrase is stark, linear, yet richly evocative of the folk languages that permeate the Egyptian literary sensibility through and through. This is perhaps the greatest difficulty that meets the English translator of Yahya Taher Abdullah's writing: How to remain faithful to his Arabic phrase with its sudden images, its peculiar elisions and repetitions, while evoking for the English-language reader the vast repertoire of literary and poetic allusion that lies close beneath the surface? How to convey the compact and remarkably elegant oral quality of his prose without resorting to the kinds of easy English colloquialisms that would empty it of its striking and highly crafted poeticism?

On the whole, I have tried to address these translation issues by taking a literal—or 'foreignizing'—approach to the text. Rather than rendering the Arabic sentence into idiomatic English, I have tried to stay close to the syntactic peculiarities of Abdullah's style, with its characteristic grammatical inversions and temporal excisions. Likewise, I have preferred to translate literally—but always with an ear to their deep poetry—the many proverbs and folk aphorisms that Abdullah weaves into his writing, rather than to look for an English equivalent, except when this equivalent was simple and obvious enough to impose itself. Finally, I have refrained, as much as possible, from resorting to explanatory strategies such as notes or interpolated clauses within the translation, to avoid marring the text with a kind of semantic utilitarianism that is entirely foreign to it. In most cases, the expression or reference in question is likely familiar to any reader with even the most basic knowledge of Islamic society; in the remaining few, the context itself suffices to convey the meaning. I have stuck to this strategy, even when the question of possible misunderstanding has arisen, preferring to allow the reader to confront what at first sight in English may appear as a kind of cultural barrier to translation. A case in point is Abdullah's deliberate use of racial or gender stereotypes—the "Cunning Jew," the "feeble-minded female," or the black domestic slave or servant: all stock figures of popular proverb or medieval romance that the author deploys in order to make a critical political point or to poke fun at the tradition itself. In spite—or perhaps because—of difficulties like these, the task has been an immensely rewarding one, and I would like to thank Tarek Abdallah, Magdi Guirguis, and Sarah al-Khodary for their invaluable help in making it so.

Modern Arabic Literature
from the American University in Cairo Press

Ibrahim Abdel Meguid *Birds of Amber* • *Distant Train*
No One Sleeps in Alexandria • *The Other Place*
Yahya Taher Abdullah *The Collar and the Bracelet*
The Mountain of Green Tea
Leila Abouzeid *The Last Chapter*
Hamdi Abu Golayyel *Thieves in Retirement*
Yusuf Abu Rayya *Wedding Night*
Ahmed Alaidy *Being Abbas el Abd*
Idris Ali *Dongola: A Novel of Nubia* • *Poor*
Ibrahim Aslan *The Heron* • *Nile Sparrows*
Alaa Al Aswany *Chicago* • *Friendly Fire* • *The Yacoubian Building*
Fadhil al-Azzawi *Cell Block Five* • *The Last of the Angels*
Hala El Badry *A Certain Woman* • *Muntaha*
Salwa Bakr *The Golden Chariot* • *The Man from Bashmour*
The Wiles of Men
Halim Barakat *The Crane*
Hoda Barakat *Disciples of Passion* • *The Tiller of Waters*
Mourid Barghouti *I Saw Ramallah*
Mohamed El-Bisatie *Clamor of the Lake* • *Houses Behind the Trees* • *Hunger*
A Last Glass of Tea • *Over the Bridge*
Mansoura Ez Eldin *Maryam's Maze*
Ibrahim Farghali *The Smiles of the Saints*
Hamdy el-Gazzar *Black Magic*
Tawfiq al-Hakim *The Essential Tawfiq al-Hakim*
Abdelilah Hamdouchi *The Final Bet*
Fathy Ghanem *The Man Who Lost His Shadow*
Randa Ghazy *Dreaming of Palestine*
Gamal al-Ghitani *Pyramid Texts* • *Zayni Barakat*
Yahya Hakki *The Lamp of Umm Hashim*
Bensalem Himmich *The Polymath* • *The Theocrat*
Taha Hussein *The Days* • *A Man of Letters* • *The Sufferers*
Sonallah Ibrahim *Cairo: From Edge to Edge* • *The Committee* • *Zaat*
Yusuf Idris *City of Love and Ashes*
Denys Johnson-Davies *The AUC Press Book of Modern Arabic Literature*
Under the Naked Sky: Short Stories from the Arab World

Said al-Kafrawi *The Hill of Gypsies*
Sahar Khalifeh *The End of Spring*
The Image, the Icon, and the Covenant • *The Inheritance*
Edwar al-Kharrat *Rama and the Dragon* • *Stones of Bobello*
Betool Khedairi *Absent*
Mohammed Khudayyir *Basrayatha: Portrait of a City*
Ibrahim al-Koni *Anubis* • *Gold Dust*
Naguib Mahfouz *Adrift on the Nile* • *Akhenaten: Dweller in Truth*
Arabian Nights and Days • *Autumn Quail* • *The Beggar*
The Beginning and the End • *Cairo Modern*
The Cairo Trilogy: Palace Walk, Palace of Desire, Sugar Street
Children of the Alley • *The Day the Leader Was Killed*
The Dreams • *Dreams of Departure* • *Echoes of an Autobiography*
The Harafish • *The Journey of Ibn Fattouma*
Karnak Café • *Khufu's Wisdom* • *Life's Wisdom* • *Midaq Alley* • *Miramar*
Mirrors • *Morning and Evening Talk* • *Naguib Mahfouz at Sidi Gaber*
Respected Sir • *Rhadopis of Nubia* • *The Search*
The Seventh Heaven • *Thebes at War* • *The Thief and the Dogs*
The Time and the Place • *Voices from the Other World* • *Wedding Song*
Mohamed Makhzangi *Memories of a Meltdown*
Alia Mamdouh *Naphtalene* • *The Loved Ones*
Selim Matar *The Woman of the Flask*
Ibrahim al-Mazini *Ten Again*
Yousef Al-Mohaimeed *Wolves of the Crescent Moon*
Ahlam Mosteghanemi *Chaos of the Senses* • *Memory in the Flesh*
Buthaina Al Nasiri *Final Night*
Ibrahim Nasrallah *Inside the Night*
Haggag Hassan Oddoul *Nights of Musk*
Abd al-Hakim Qasim *Rites of Assent*
Somaya Ramadan *Leaves of Narcissus*
Lenin El-Ramly *In Plain Arabic*
Ghada Samman *The Night of the First Billion*
Rafik Schami *Damascus Nights*
Khairy Shalaby *The Lodging House*
Miral al-Tahawy *Blue Aubergine* • *The Tent*
Bahaa Taher *Love in Exile*
Fuad al-Takarli *The Long Way Back*
Latifa al-Zayyat *The Open Door*